The Persian Wedding

Michael Flay

Polar Books

Polar Books
First published in 2015
By Polar Books UK, Greenways,
Bowbridge Lane, Prestbury, Cheltenham,
Gloucestershire, GL52 3BL, England

Typeset by M. Rules Ltd., London
Printed in Great Britain by
Berforts Information Press, Stevenage.

All rights reserved

Copyright © Michael Flay 2015

ISBN 978-0-9536309-5-0

*This book is sold subject to the condition that it shall not,
by way of trade or otherwise, be lent, resold, hired out or
otherwise circulated without the publisher's prior consent
in any form of binding or cover other than that in which it
is published and without a similar condition including this
condition being imposed on the subsequent purchaser.*

*No part of this publication may be reproduced,
stored in a retrieval system, or transmitted in any form
or by any means, electronic, mechanical, photocopying,
recording or otherwise, without the prior permission
of the publishers*

PART ONE

The sun hung queer in the sky. For a month now it had burned constant, a new thing, the summer lay hot all around. He was glad, he'd wanted to change. He was young, things lay behind.

It was a summer evening. The house stood at the end of a long gravel drive where bushes came swelling out on each side, cut back only roughly. Fading sun was caught between creepers with blue flowers that climbed the pale brickwork. Sash windows were open, and there was a sound of foreign voices. It was a place for students. The house had a balance and poise, Georgian, distinct, there in the countryside. At the back a lawn sloped gently downwards to a wooden fence, wound over in brambles and wild plants. Beyond, a slight incline led across fields to the river and railway, remote behind distant trees. For days the heat had held everything in suspense; even the sun seemed grey, hazed over. But in the evenings sometimes a slight breeze came and the air moved again, just.

The girl was coming out of the white doorway at the front of the house. She paused and slipped a little as she crossed the step, looking sideways uncertainly, but with the pride to cover her brief lapse. Her black hair reached thickly to her shoulders; she moved quite briskly, with a warm grace. Now she came out into the evening, obviously foreign, with her dark hair and warm eyes, easy movement. She stood still, forgetful of herself, looking to see him, shading her eyes.

THE PERSIAN WEDDING

He saw her from the far edge of the lawn where he was waiting in the shade of a bush. He noticed quickly her dark hair and her eyes which looked at him now with warmth and playfulness. He was glad she had come; he had waited for her all day, through his other activities. Those were just obstructions until he could be with her. Now a physical gladness filled him, an excitement without thought.

It was a different world here in the evening light, on the lawn at the edge of a small wood, like a coppice, in the house's grounds. He stood up, smiling, put his arm briefly round her, while she leaned towards him. He was proud to be there with her. She made him feel rich and strong in himself, changed. They turned their backs on the house and walked up a path towards the wood. The foreign chatter from the house fell away as they walked and it grew darker as the big trees began to hang overhead.

The couple paused, small insects flew about in the dusk. He didn't know what effect he had on her – he just felt her physical and near, she was gravitating towards him, inevitably, in some way given up to him. No-one had ever approached him so closely before. His blood melted towards hers.

She looked at him now, smiling, quiet. Sometimes she would tease him. He saw the teasing challenge in her eyes. He was always wondering at her – how could she be like this, so much what he wanted? She was splendid and warm. Taking her against his body was to melt out into a movement of blood; she gave herself to the flow without resisting, or perhaps being able to. The strength of it all bewildered him – he found himself smiling at times with the pleasure of it, when he was alone. Both of them were separate from the others, in their own world and flow. It was like being asleep, but in the sleep was a wakefulness at odds with the ordinary world, a vital impulse against it.

She looked at him laughing.

'So, when will you come to Persia? I don't believe you will come.' She spoke teasingly but with real fear he wouldn't come after all. She was always disguising her fear with laughter. It was worrying them both, how he could go there. He looked at her quickly.

'I'll come – soon after you've gone back. I must get some money to come. I will be paid for working here, at this college.' He hadn't any money, until he was paid for the summer teaching. She looked satisfied with this.

'Make sure you do come.'

He was nervous of the strange land, tentative. What would he find there? She would help him. He trusted her. But what work could he do? He pushed the deliberation about these colder things aside.

'You can find a job there. It will be easy for you.' She seemed anxious for a moment, then smiled. 'I can help you, all my friends will help.' She was pleased to imagine the activity on his behalf. He gently touched her warm black hair that fascinated him.

The hot evening enclosed them – she walked close to him with a different warmth. He was excited with her beside him. There was a new strength and fullness now leading into the future. The path had wound back on itself. Now they crossed the unkempt driveway, like a country track, rutted with a line of grass along its centre, a verge, and climbed up a small bank covered in thick grass. A small church once belonging to the house stood secluded behind a line of ragged bushes, there were tennis courts. The place was wild. The bushes bulged out unrestrained, there were brambles, white flowers that screened them. The old house was only a short distance away, they saw its lights, the edges of its roof tiles rising dimly, lit attic windows. It was all new, unknown.

He helped her to climb the bank; she slipped in her smooth soled platform shoes. They had been here often before; now he sat down on the grass near the top of the bank and she lay on her side, turned towards him. She saw him sitting in the dark, half hidden, though they were next to each other. Everything was changed for him now – he was lapsed with her into the night and these grounds, alert only to the woman and the place in a strange, peaceful vividness he hadn't known before. They were both drawn on into this quiet alertness. It was their world. She pulled up handfuls of grass, put them in a heap, a jacket on top.

'Look, I've made a pillow for us.' She looked at him proudly, gently confident. Things lay ahead, they would deal with them, make it through, use this force.

Some evenings, late, they went for a drive. In the daytime the usual teaching went on. The work was always distant, insignificant. This night it was the same as usual. He sat in the small college van, in front of the house, waiting. She had gone upstairs to fetch some biscuits and fruit. He saw her, through a tall window, as she crossed the upper landing; she was musing. She struck him as delicate but also strong in her elegance and alive; there was the proud, mocking beauty of her that he loved, also her quiet sensitivity. She loved to feel they were in a separate world together as he drove. She handed him a biscuit, familiar, touching him as she reached across.

The drive was dusty with powdered white gravel. It hadn't rained for weeks. The headlights picked out rising dust, the brambles leaning into the roadway. They turned down a narrow lane towards the river. The windows were open and cooler air rushed in, a welcome change after the still, dense heat of the daytime.

Tonight they turned into the yard of a small railway station, a halt at the end of the road. The place was deserted, they often came, no-one but them came there at night, no trains stopped. They sat on the steps of a footbridge that crossed the tracks. Heat beat up where they sat. A few lights shone on posts up the platform, a horse rustled in a nearby field. They were talking, about what she had done in England at this private college, before she met him, about her parents and Persia. He listened to her, Persia was mysterious to him as she talked, he couldn't imagine it clearly. He was here, with her now, on the station steps and the talking stopped, everything was silent. As they kissed each other in the distance across some fields they could hear cars on a main road. Things were their way, nothing else counted.

She was leaning gently against him and they were quiet. Then, she began.

'In Persia, we couldn't do this. My father – if he knew ...!' She tailed off, laughing, but there was worry in the laugh as well. He looked up, wondering.

'Why not? Why would he mind?' He asked the question half lazily, half wanting to know the answer.

The night and heat were so strongly about them, it was hard to imagine anything else, anywhere, existing, having an effect. There were the fir trees opposite, lining the station drive, a signal light glowed on the tracks west in the distance, here was the hot dark evening. They were together. What else was there? How could anything else count or come to affect them?

'I don't know,' she began. 'My father ...' She stopped, thinking about the words to use. He listened to her with a wondering pleasure, touched in a deep intoxicated way, asleep in her warmth. What kind of father could she have? And, in any case, he wasn't bothered, knew he had had one of the best educations possible, didn't feel daunted. Who could gainsay him, he was confident.

He saw her eyes looking at him in the night, they were gleaming, there was her black hair so thick and dark, foreign in its richness and colour. She was confident too. She felt in the same world with him as the darkness, heat, the trees behind her. They were both there. The words and explanations weren't important. She challenged him in a vital way, to move on with her. She spoke gently, looking at him all the time.

'We can manage ... but what will my grandmother say?' The idea of her grandmother meeting the foreign man amused her. He imagined an old woman in black. The night air closed round them as she spoke. They stopped talking again. He was optimistic, why should anyone make difficulties, there was nothing wrong with himself, no-one could object.

They'd go back to the house. Inside the van it was hot and dark. He could feel her touching him gently as he drove, melting his blood. It wasn't far to get back. The old walls of the house lit up white ahead. No-one was about. It always seemed the world was theirs. The air was still again as they got out of the van, shutting the doors quietly, treading lightly on the gravel surface. The air smelt of the trees in the wood nearby. The place was utterly relaxed and at ease, isolated in its own stillness. Now they separated. The women slept in rooms in one part of the house, cut off from the rest.

Sometimes they drove in another direction. There were lanes where the foliage grew out to scrape the van doors, tall, white flowers hung out in front of them. Once they'd suddenly come to gates where there were security units each side. A nuclear warning sign hung in some fir trees; he pulled in, they lit cigarettes, paused. A small, white stream foamed out fast below a hedge, gates opened jerkily, quiet in the country, a black car emerged, dwindled up the lane. A man eyed them in the van, came across, advised moving on.

She pushed the map towards him. He checked it out.

'Some kind of research centre – nuclear.' He remembered here'd been leakages into local brooks; under the ground warheads were tested in deep, contained explosions. Even a relative of his had worked there, gone to a stately home further west to liaise with the military and surveillance intelligence.

'Maybe the king will buy this stuff.' She was smiling. It was unusual for her to make comments of this sort. 'He buys a lot from you.' She leaned across to kiss him on the mouth.

He moved the van, back up the lanes where no-one seemed to go but them, the foliage came together behind, the plants swished white flowers as they passed, the heat burned. The research centre was gone, they were pressing on further into their own world.

THE PERSIAN WEDDING

Now he watched her go up the elegant staircase, wondering over her. Who was she that she was all the time so close to him? He was released now, into a finer world, his life would be with hers. He stood in the small side porch, looking out. The moon lit up the gravel drive and square in front of the house, the trees stood up opposite. He had never felt so happy as now.

He climbed the side stairs to his room. The sun had been shining in on it all afternoon and the heat had stayed, trapped. For weeks it had been hot and heavy, no rain. In the night the walls radiated heat. He stood looking out of the fully open sash window. In the distance a few houses were visible, by their lights – otherwise nothing. He would be going to Persia, in any case, things here wouldn't matter anymore.

He took off his clothes and lay between the sheets. Even with the window open it was still too hot. He lay there, thinking about the day.

There was a tap at the door. At night she would sometimes come, briefly, just to see if he was still there. She was always afraid he would be gone. She came of her own accord – he had never asked her. So he was always surprised to hear the knock, pleased and excited. He opened the door a little, cautiously, quickly.

'It's me – can I come in?' She came in, kissed him gently. He stood there with a towel draped round him, half-asleep. She smiled and looked at him for reassurance, still dressed in her daytime clothes.

Sometimes she climbed into bed with him, lay close. They would talk.

'You know, I don't do like English girls. Only when I am married. You see, we are Moslem.'

He looked back at her, smiling.

'You can be as you like.'

'Yes, and in a week I am gone.'

It was true, she would leave then. It was hard to believe this place and mode would end. She was worried.

'You will come soon – in two months at least?'

He knew he would go there, there was no alternative. Nearly she had stayed. Her father had gone, last minute to English colleges, ignored their deadlines, hoped to deal and fix a study place. But he was too late, nothing was available. So she was to go back, go on with university in Tehran. It was all random and strange. Maybe the father wanted her back. Though there was prestige to have children studying in England.

She looked tired, for a moment, then elated.

'You can get a job.' She was laughing, the idea of him at work. She drew him softly towards her, in the bed. She would never stay for long. She touched him lightly before she left, leant gently against him as they both stood at the door. The hot dark air hung at the window, beat in off the walls. She kissed him possessively. He slipped back between the sheets as the door closed, full of strong love for her. Something was coming to pass for both of them, they were caught up in a vivid movement that bore them along. Soon she would have to go back and he would have to plan his departure, to follow hers.

It was the evening before she would leave. They sat in his room together, on the floor, their backs to a small settee. He stroked her fine black hair and wondered again how she could be like this. She amazed him, by being what he wanted. Her bracelet and a scarf were on a small stool, she had left them there a few days before. She liked to leave her things in his room. She turned to him softly.

'What can we do in Iran?' She paused, tentatively, then continued. 'We could be married there ...' She was looking at him to know his response. They had often spoken about these things. He felt his blood stirring with pleasure and pride.

'Yes, you must ask your parents.' He knew this was the procedure she wanted to follow. He didn't know how things were done, trusted her to deal with procedure. They lay together in a close warmth, happy with this freedom. The house, the land around, the warm night air, themselves, were all bound together in a flow he hadn't known before he met her.

She was leaving now. They sat on the seat in the hall where they had often sat before. The seat was different now, this was the end of this place for them. The sun lit up the gravel of the drive, the white doorway, fell in on the stone floor, lighting it in brilliant streaks. There was the grassy bank beyond the bushes, where they had talked over plans. Now it was ending; they would be in different places.

They stood, hugged each other. The taxi had arrived. The door closed, she was waving. The car was moving away. He watched the white gravel dust float up in powdery clouds, obscuring her as the tyres moved over the driveway, the taxi turned the corner. She was gone, then. The next move was his responsibility.

After six hours on the plane she would be somewhere he had no knowledge of, there would be a party with her parents and relatives to welcome her back. She would be in a house and city he couldn't imagine, or if he did it would be wrong. He'd been in her room, there'd been a Persian magazine on her bed. The colours were garish, cheap print. A man with a moustache had looked back at him from the cover, inside were a few cartoons; there was the odd Persian script he couldn't understand, pictures of national stars, the King and his family. The King was often in English magazines, a rich celebrity, royal with a cherished family.

His thoughts had speculated as the girl packed. What was the place he'd go to? One of her Persian friends had once showed him a trick pack of matches – she'd opened it and out sprung a paper penis and the girls had laughed. There'd be oil rigs, deserts, he'd seen pictures; now came a series of images, the King was suspect too. But it all was extraneous, it didn't inform, he knew nothing, would find out only there.

THE PERSIAN WEDDING

He watched her pack. Her movements seemed to speak to him, to answer his needs in vital ways. He only wanted her, mysteriously. She knew he was looking at her and was pleased, smiled at him. She would see her parents and she loved this man. Good. She was happy as she packed. She wasn't worried by any thought of future problems; she trusted to a happy outcome, his arrival, that was all she wanted.

The plane was flying low in the darkness. Down below shone the orange lights of the strange city; he wondered what was down there. The plane twisted and tilted, they were lining up for the landing. It was three in the morning. The jerking and dropping, like going down stairs, carried on. The plane smelt of aviation fuel, sweet, a slight exhaust fume came in with the air fan. There'd been a stop in Moscow, it was a Soviet plane, cheap ticket but expensive to him, red stars on towers, a Russian had shared vodka with him in the stopover bar.

The plane hit the runway. It was winter now. Snow banked up on the edges of the runways rushed white and vague past the windows. The plane slowed then turned, to taxi towards the berth. It was queer, three a.m., Tehran.

Outside, on top of the mobile steps, he looked round at the new country for the first time. He was excited. All was blank and unrevealed. It was a usual airport landscape, dirty; the air felt different, cold and sharp with an ice edge. He was elated, pleased when he put his foot on the tarmac – he had come here, to Persia. He didn't know what to expect. A bus drove him to the terminal. He passed through modern doorways into a baggage hall, old, wooden, to collect his bags. The place was spartan, unfinished. Then he moved into a modern hall that opened to the outside. He felt exposed.

There would be no-one to meet him, he knew. He would have to wait until at least seven in the morning before he could telephone. Those were her instructions. She didn't know he was coming on that exact flight. Sliding doors led out into the night, freezing air blew in as they opened and shut. It was black outside, nothing was visible. He was enjoying the fact of arriving, having come at all.

Suddenly there was a stir, army men were tensing up. From a side door came a group of suited men, he heard a drawl in American and too familiar English, from England privileged tones. The military men walked beside them, fast, they were away in cars. They looked like men he'd seen before, blurred. There was the black car, he recalled another at the English nuclear site, an obscure figure inside, vague shapes ran things, remote, wherever you were. Sellers were all over and here the oil money was to covet, a market, evil goods, buy and sell, all. He saw the men vague and gone, through the glass. The lounge fell back to a dawn suspense, quiet, people asleep. A man next to him was pointing, with a grin.

'For the King. They've come for him. Military helpers, sellers.' He spat on the ground. 'He flies them in, in his own planes.' The visitor would have spat too, but he didn't want to draw attention to himself. As it was, an officer was eyeing the Persian who had made the remarks. Things subsided back, waiting.

He sat on a circular seat, looked about. A few men in blue overalls were sweeping up. Some army officers in thick overcoats stood heavily in one corner of the lounge. If you were from the West they were on your side. They caused him no trouble.

The hours slid away. Outside it was getting lighter. Peaks of mountains were revealed in dim pink sun light straight ahead as the dark began to lift. The day was becoming ordinary after the seclusion of night. Women in black robes sat in groups, a few dressed in western fashions. Someone touched his arm silently – a black swathed woman smiled, handed him his glove which he'd dropped. He was starting to feel tired, the details of the ordinary day bothered him, he wanted to sleep, it was jet lag and he'd been up all night.

He'd shake it off but in phases he saw details over-vivid, surreal. There were braids on the officers' peaked hats, they wore shades now, had slung them on, more ominous. The arrival of the men in suits had aroused them.

Then another was coming through, fat, there was a hustle about him of military men. It was royal to royal, he'd be taken to the palace, they'd have a feast. The visitor recognised him, a fat prince from England, used as a business envoy. Only here he had a role of selling things. He'd been in the army too, brief, trained as an officer, plump and protected, a royal. His thick face turned this way and that. Now he was through, hidden over by the security systems. His wake subsided, he'd never been, he was invisible.

It was six o'clock. He would telephone now, even before the time she'd set, impatient. He moved across to the phones set on the wall, put his head into a plastic cowl before dialling. Her father spoke sleepily. He knew he should conceal his identity. He asked for Zohre. She was answering tentatively. She couldn't speak openly because of her parents, it was obvious.

'Allo'

'Hello – I'm at the airport, here.' He heard her voice tremble and change slightly.

'I'm coming – stay there. Don't move.' She replied briefly, not to arouse her father's suspicions. 'Just wait.' She was afraid he would disappear.

He sat down on the seat again, very pleased. Now they would be together. It didn't matter how long he'd have to wait. He had told her he was here. He knew she'd come. That was fixed. The mountains glimmered in the queer pink light with a grey haze below, visible through the flat glass of the terminal. It was strange, the concealments, in England a girl could have a boyfriend stay in her parents' home if she wanted, but here that wasn't so. In the country house and its grounds, the lanes around, they had done as they chose. The thoughts came by, he let them drift.

He went to a counter and bought tea. It came black and in a small glass, tasted good, foreign and sharp. A few workmen made friendly space for him at the bar. An hour passed. Then came a message for him over the loudspeaker. He walked to the desk to take the call.

'I had to wait til my parents had gone out – I'm coming now. I told them your call was about a key at the university – I'd gone off with it! So now just don't move.'

'I'm here. It's fine.'

It hardly registered that she must wait til her parents had gone, he just accepted it. Things were vague, he didn't think much about them.

He saw her before she saw him, coming across a crowded lounge. Her black hair was shorter – she was moving hurriedly in between crowded groups of people. He felt in a daze, jet lag was deepening and the new details were a confusion. Did she still love him? He looked at her for a clue. She kissed him on both cheeks and he kissed her in reply. She would want to know if he still loved her. They looked at each other as if they couldn't believe this was happening. She held onto his arm, tightly. There had been delays, his failed efforts to earn more money to bring.

She talked quickly, looking at him all the time intent, as if he might vanish.

'I had to wait for my parents to go out,' she repeated. 'If they knew you were here ... you must be careful, both of us.' She didn't finish. Then she began again. 'Now we will go – to the city. And to your hotel.' She was smiling, had made these arrangements for them both. What was familiar, the place, its procedures, to her were the reverse to him. Both needed the other's help in the new situation. It was all unfamiliar for them, how to move forward. She had a plan, how her parents would be won round.

'Shall we go – to the hotel?' She looked at him, pleased, but uncertain about taking charge. It was her country and he knew nothing about it. She must help him now, understand his needs. She had everything, he had nothing at his disposal.

But her parents hung over her too, a means to what she had and could do.

They walked out of the sliding doors for the first time. He breathed the freezing air outside. It was the new land. Daylight shone strange, diffused and hazy and it was cold. They got into a taxi. On their left a waste area scattered with shallow snow, yellow earth poking through, held vague frames of unfinished apartment blocks. The car turned into a broad carriageway, jammed up with slow moving vehicles. Always, further off, were the snow covered mountain peaks, blurred by the dusty daylight haze, exhausts. Zohre leaned against him. They didn't speak. She held his hand as the car moved on. He was still unused to her.

There was also the outer landscape to relate to – the new context. He looked out of the window, confused. He was tired and he didn't want to be, the jet lag jerked images in over detail, then he was seeing as things were. The traffic was dense and increased as they got further into the city. There were intersections where eight lanes crossed eight other lanes, at random, cars swerved, edged over. A few pickups had goats or sheep tethered in the open back.

He took it all in fast, his attention was with her, her hand resting on his also. Outside everything was dusty, cars were covered in snow, then dust and a hazy light made the atmosphere weird. Air hung heavy with exhaust fumes, coloured blue grey. Unfinished blocks of apartments lined the road in disorder. Buildings were put up, incomplete, non embedded on scrap land.

The cars packed in together along the road, moving fast. There were several limousines, chauffeur driven, running silently, these were common like broken off parts of a US president's cavalcade, dispersed. Everywhere space was taken up, cars, buildings, as if dumped down at random, unembedded and laid on.

She was squeezing his hand. The outside context dropped his spirits. Now they were in the centre of the city: garish versions of western style shops and outlets were squeezed together in rough new developments. Haphazard buildings massed together in crowds. It looked temporary, like hallucinations of disorder, shortly to vanish. Yet the city was actual. A few oil tankers ran past, khaki and matt like military vehicles, dirty sides stained with the liquid wealth that made this kind of city possible.

He looked at Zohre, wondering what she felt. He was isolated in the revelation of the city though she was there. She seemed in a dream; the city had little to do with her, except in so far as it unfolded itself outside a car's windows. And she lived in a quieter, more pleasant zone, he knew. They couldn't go there.

The traffic moved off again, the car turned right into a quieter road. Here the pace wasn't so frenzied. Trees stood at the edge of a gulley with water rushing white and snow was ploughed into heaps along the edges of the road. A small hotel was nearby. The taxi was gone, the journey so far was over. His former life was at a distance. Things were different, he felt slightly ashamed of his intense reactions; for sure fatigue and jet lag were factors and these seemed to be getting worse, not wearing off. He felt shy, couldn't explain. It wasn't an ideal way to feel.

They crossed the road, went into the hotel opposite. The interior was dark and quiet, basically furnished. A young man at the desk joked with them both, friendly, handing over the room key. The room itself was on the first floor, overlooked the street. Zohre didn't follow him in; she waited, instead, on the landing just below, where a few old armchairs had been left. He was surprised.

'Why don't you come in?'

'I can't unless I ask him.' She pointed to the desk. She went off, he could hear her talking in Persian, the rise and fall of the mysterious words. She could persuade people easily, he believed.

'Yes, for a minute, I can go in.'

Inside the room it was strange, knowing the man downstairs didn't want them together in there and was waiting for her to come out. It was against custom for her to be in there with him. She kissed him, knowing she had to go out again, a constraint. She looked at him questioningly, wanting to be given some direction, knowing he must mind they couldn't be together in there or really speak.

'It's not for long. Then we can go to your flat.' She had arranged a place for him to stay. 'In a few days time.'

She could tell he was tired. She had a plan.

'You must rest. I will go home, to change, and come again in two hours. It's not far from here.' She wanted to change her appearance for him. She had had no time to dress as she wanted before going to the airport, she'd been in a hurry. She'd been careful not to make her parents suspicious, by dressing finely. Also they didn't like her to wear much make up if she went out by herself. Before she could leave there was a knock on the door. The man at the desk was asking her definitely to come out of the room, polite and humorous. She left and he heard her voice in the hall as she went out. She didn't know much about jet lag, he would be feeling worse after two hours, it was hard to adjust.

He was in the room. The journey itself was over, then. No-one he knew had been to this place. Already it was unexpected, there were halts and delays, the phone call her father answered, the room she couldn't enter. Whereas he wanted it different at once. She would explain later, how it was all to be. He didn't know. He felt oblique, at the side of what was usual, stripped down. There was nothing for him in reserve here whereas she had her home. He trusted her entirely but for some reason things seemed out of balance, the city was a different context, complicated and unexpected.

He was at once asleep. It seemed like he'd slept for no more than a minute when he realised the phone was ringing next to the bed. He felt in a total daze now, even worse after the deep sleep, stunned.

'Allo – your friend is downstairs.' The man at the desk spoke in slow English.

'I'm coming.' He looked in the mirror, decided his

exhausted appearance couldn't be changed. He should have shaved, washed but had fallen asleep instead. He wanted to feel entirely different, alert. Now, in a daze, he left the room. It was comic, disturbing, to feel so awful.

She was there, sitting on a chair on the landing. She looked beautiful to him; her black hair softly covered the sides of her face, while her eyes, clear and alert, watched him approach. She sat still, waiting, anxious he should like to be with her, elegant in her grey dress. Her brown eyes, opaque, were sweeping over him.

'Did you sleep?'

He nodded and she lifted her face to his, to be kissed. She looked at him warmly and for a long time, then turned away abashed.

They'd go out, into the city. She had decided beforehand where she'd take him. He hung back nervous from the city outside, in restraint. He was trying to get a grip on himself but the movement of the plane was still inside him; now and then the room seemed to lurch upwards, climbing, then fell back. Colours were strange, off-focus.

'Let's go out' she said. She wanted him to go with her into the streets, eat somewhere. She needed to place him in her habitual world, to reassure herself in the new, unaccustomed activity. And, anyway, they couldn't stay together in the room. She'd connect him up with her outside life. That was her aim.

Outside she hailed cars – apart from ordinary taxis private cars would stop, give lifts, earn money that way. A new pick up truck stopped. The driver was young, obsequious to the girl. She told him directions. Now the city street opened up as they turned into an eight lane boulevard; the traffic pressed round closely, braked at intersections, cars halted in queer positions, crossing each other, fish curves, angles. Modern blocks, rows of crudely decorated smaller shops, western style in white concrete cubes lined the street. He wound the window down and the cold air seemed thin.

THE PERSIAN WEDDING

A weak bright sun shone, lighting up the dust and haze, spreading a white light unhealthily over the cars, heaps of dirty snow, crowds. In the distance the mountains always pushed up, tempting, quiet, remote beyond the haze. She was squashed against him in the front of the van. This was all normal for her, perhaps. But she turned to him.

'Usually I go in the car – with our driver.' She seemed to be liking the new freedom.

The van moved on and he tried to quiet his senses down. A few glimpses of a different time struck him as the car passed along, slow in the unending jam of cars between the concrete buildings. An old man stood with several goats up a side alley, next to cages with chickens inside. Groups of men, swathed up, stood ominous at certain corners with police opposite. A few entrances had a fierce fire burning, intense like a locomotive firebox.

'They are baker's fires', she was laughing, pleased to tell him about the new things.

He wondered where she was taking him. She hadn't said. Now she turned to him.

'Perhaps we'll see some of my girlfriends. They'll wonder who you are. But I told everyone you were coming.' She caught his arm as she spoke and they crossed the road, stopping between the lanes of cars, moving on until finally across.

There was a low modern building ahead, luxurious, set back from the road, slightly below it. You went down ramps, there was a kind of brief garden, scattered with snow. He took in the sign, quickly, Iran-America Society. He was getting more alert now, guarded. It wasn't a place he would have chosen to come to. But she had brought him here, perhaps, thinking he would like a western atmosphere. And, in any case, she came often, it was a place partly for students.

Yet who was here? There were several men in suits, sellers at tables, he heard the US intonation, it was business deals, even government business. Zohre had sat him at a table and gone off to get food from a self-service counter. He was thinking. It was a habit. He didn't want to think this way. The thoughts annoyed him. Yet he went on. The building was a way to hide the real relation between America and Iran. The Shah here was maintained in power by the American state. He bought American warplanes, tanks, weapons. American experts gave security advice. American businesses took big profits from deals done, more than they'd get at home or in Europe. England collaborated with the States. All this was fact.

She was coming back, carrying a tray. The perceptions got in his way as far as Zohre was concerned. What was the place to her? She saw it differently maybe, part of a daily landscape, a place to go, drink coffee, eat lunch, meet friends. But she didn't always reveal herself. Beneath her air of acceptance was sometimes a tension which she tried to hide or be brave about. Once – for months – she couldn't eat meals with her parents without feeling sick. She had told him this laughingly, back in England, as if it wasn't important. Her father had taken her to doctors, spent a lot of money.

She was looking round.

'People talk – about the Americans' – she lowered her voice – 'and the King. But it's just talk, it doesn't make anything happen. A lot of people talk.' Another girl was coming to their table, one of Zohre's friends. 'Come with us – for lunch- he has just come.' She talked excitedly and laughing to her friend. The friend was drawing photographs from her bag.

'My boyfriend – he is in Europe, Italy, studying architecture.' A tall man with black hair stood in the sun in Florence, in Pisa. She explained each situation shown. The three of them sat looking at the photographs, talking and laughing. The young women were very attractive to him, with their black hair, elegance and laughter. Zohre turned to him, touched his arm, intimately.

'Shall we go to another café?'

'Yes – I must go, to the American library here.' Her friend picked up a pile of books. They walked along a ramp, into a cultural centre where the library was.

'Look, look, there are English events too.' A few posters for British cultural shows, talks were on a wall, they had rooms here too. British weapons were popular with the Shah, there were the same sellers, deals, business trade offs, reciprocal. The Shah had leant Britain billions to help their financial crisis. What was it, he wondered, that the Shah wanted to protect the country from? What were the weaponry, the spy networks, the alliances geared to exclude, keep out? The sellers were consolidating, some collaboration in an unannounced plan was under way.

'Just sit with Jali. I will take these books to the library. I told my parents so.' She smiled at him. 'So I told the truth.'

At once Jali was speaking. She spoke clear, fast. She had been walking in the road. It wasn't the capital city. She was with a boy, a fellow student. Suddenly there was a car slowing beside them, evening sun spilt tree shadows across the asphalt. Men were walking alongside, pulled the boy away. She was pushed into the police car. A man was leering,

'So who are you, Shah's dolly?' She was wearing jeans and a pullover, a headscarf across her hair. She was protesting,

'Why have you stopped me, why?'

'We have to know, what are you doing here. Perhaps you are a prostitute or troublemaker. We must check you all over.'

She was pushed into a small cell behind the brick wall of a compound. Over the entry gate stood a sentry with a machine gun on a tripod. All the local police stations were like this. The King had a standardised pattern he favoured following a consultant's suggestion.

A policeman was grinning in.

'You do poses like on American television. Strip off to your pants and dance? Or you twist about, sex with everyone, like an English girl?' Now he was ominous, a woman's face also poked at the grill, squashed and sneery.

'Or you plot with your boyfriend against the King? Plotters walk late in the streets.' The grill was banged shut.

She sat on a stool in the room. A few wires poked from bare brick, there was dust in a corner. The place was cut off, remote as an embassy room, no-one knew what went on.

The grill was banged open.

'Papers? And now take off your pullover. Sit there nice for me while we check. Go on, everyone wants to see you strip and it's what you like, are used to. The King doesn't want Persian girls to be sluts and whores.'

She was sitting on. Then there came a banging open of the door, the policewoman stood, holding the papers. The man was pressing behind, threatening.

'So, your father is an officer in the King's army. That is good, a good thing. You must tell him what we can do. I am sure he is a loyal officer. And now you can go.'

She was turned out, alone, into the deserted street. A dim streetlight showed the road petering out into a dusty area of wasteland and then arid stretches of sandy earth. A few broken trees poked out of the ground and in a cluster on the edge of town new military vehicles were stored, paintwork waxy with preservative; there were tank barrels shining dull but with cardboard covers tied across the opening. It was like new televisions in boxes, the things gleamed unused, waiting to be switched on, a kind of innocent new cleanliness hung around. She wouldn't go near there but she could see on the cardboard covers small Union Jacks and the Rolls Royce military engine logos, marketing come here, to the military storage area.

With a start, turning in the road, she saw a small mound that seemed to stir. Running over, she saw her boyfriend, his face streaked with blood, and he was moving twisted.

'It was as usual. A King's beating.' He turned aside to vomit in the road. She was wiping his face and after a while they could move. They'd sit in an alleyway and wait until dawn, take the bus back to the city.

*

He listened as she spoke. She smiled at him.

'Now he is in Italy, studying. And I am all right too. But you have to take care here.' Zohre was coming back. She eyed her friend, quizzically.

'I was telling him – something about Iran.'

'There would be many things to tell.'

The girls were silent. It was frustrating. How did you live here, your family was here, things went on. They were both wondering.

Zohre was continuing.

'And with the telling nothing changes.' She seemed annoyed, why say negative things. She wanted to make something happy happen, the incident was behind.

They were passing more closed off buildings. There were trees, small gardens visible through security gates with grills. They looked foreign and incongruous here. Suddenly, with a shock, he noticed one building was flying the English flag. A small plaque on the wall showed the place as an embassy. It was queer, he felt far off: what was in there had nothing to do with him and he had come here to get away from it. A thin man was visible at the window, twisted at a cabinet, then he vanished. Cars were arriving, black glass, vaguely he saw remote shapes like those at the airport getting out, they were in fast, blurring past with the military at their sides, it was quiet and discreet, important but not to be noticed. Zohre was walking, chatting to her friend, the embassies were nothing to her, she held them in contempt.

Next to the cultural centre the American flag also flew in a yard in front of another high alien building. There were trees too, an expensive fountain, switched off in the snow. The windows were blacked out and in the road outside stood more long cars with dark glass. Someone was calling out, a car was starting up, there were British voices as well. He was far off, these men had to save up for nothing, moved in an oblique world of privilege in which he was no-one. The minister would be high, separate. No-one was anything outside the circles, deals circulated, equipment was delivered, influences applied, a kind of parallel universe operated for a limited, dominant group.

The men were jinking by, expensive, suits, winners and aware of it. He felt thousands of miles off, walking jetlagged in the road without power. Zohre was turning back to him, took his hand below her coat, the embassies were away now and they were turning into a restaurant, a cake shop.

Everything was lit up green, some of the cakes were green. Downstairs a man in a black jacket and tie, elegant, ushered them round a bend into a large low-ceilinged room. Young people sat at big tables, on large soft bench seats in alcoves and in the central part of the room. Lighting was low, with the green motif. The family in Iran kept a control on its daughters. But after school or college courses they could come here, meet friends. Once there'd been a book fight down there and since then bags had to be left upstairs. The waiters had rushed round, the place had been subverted. The room seemed slightly furtive, guilty.

Outside cars still swamped the carriageway. The white light was curious to him, lighting tiny things up, over intense. A toxic haze hung ghost blue above the cars. They walked up the pavement. At a road junction he suddenly noticed six men wrapped in black robes, leaning against a wall. Their faces were covered except for the eyes and one was intoning, regular, rhythmic. The eyes had a suspended, watchful look that was in part not comprehending, also malevolent. They were jeering at the city with their eyes, reciting verses against it. At a small distance from them stood a group of policemen, just watching now and then. They were wearing guns strapped across their chests, white gloves and dark glasses. The girl was skirting the group, keeping a distance. They were eyeing her with distaste, her short coat, uncovered hair, one started a muttering.

'Who are they?' he asked her. She looked a little startled, then laughed.

'I think they are – what is the word – gypsies. Or maybe they are men with no work. Or they could be the Moslems. They come in from the country and try to cause trouble. I don't like them, they are backward people.'

'Why are they here?'

'I don't know. They come in from far away, then the police tell them to go back. Sometimes they round them up, put them in vans.' It was facts, features of daily life, you dealt with it.

They got in a taxi to go back to the hotel. They car crawled through the blocked streets. When they arrived it was early, six p.m.; the white light was fading down into dusk, air icing up, hard to breathe. They sat on the landing, talking. He liked it alone with her in the quieter space. There would be a lot to talk about. Now they would begin, perhaps.

But she looked at her watch.

'I must go now', she said, smiling, sudden.

'But it's just six.' He was taken aback.

'I have to go – for my parents. My father – we must always eat together. And then I have to stay at home in the house.' It was a fact for her, that she had to go home. This was a difficult surprise. She had never mentioned it in England. There, the evenings had been unrestrained. Here things were subject to limitations he didn't understand yet. Why should she go back now? She looked vulnerable as she stood there, very young for a moment. He knew she didn't want him to make a fuss or argue; her eyes asked him to let her go. He accepted she had to leave. But he was upset. Why couldn't they be together now? He had come to Tehran, it had been hard for him to come, a big event. Now she was constrained by something in the background that hadn't been present in England. It was the father, a family. But he knew he must be patient, understand her circumstances.

'I will come tomorrow, at half past eight', she told him. Briefly he was sad, even annoyed she was going, obeyed so readily. But he knew the feeling was unfair. She kissed him, in the lounge, before she went – she murmured as she put her mouth to his. An old woman in black looked at them curiously; she had appeared suddenly, round a corner, cleaning. As the girl left he heard her say something in Persian to the old woman in reply.

The first day here was ended, then, strange, as if it had been cut short. He moved out of his haze of arriving. The day seemed to have had no beginning, to have gone on indefinitely and in fact two days had run into one. He knew he needed to be alert. She would need to inform him how things were. Some kind of labyrinth had opened. Yet she was proud. She wouldn't want to admit to him limits in what she was allowed or not and maybe she saw no limits, just facts in which she lived like many Persian girls. For some too, the facts were harder. She didn't want him to think of her as constrained, controlled. The day had accumulated to a point, not penetrable. She knew everything here, he knew little. He was very glad to have come, be with her again, it was sure.

He went to sleep in the strange room. He woke, suddenly. It was two in the morning. Through the thin curtain he could see the unfamiliar snow gleaming under the yellow streetlights; the city was shut down, deserted. He ate some biscuits, went back to sleep. The phone rang suddenly as it had done the day before, woke him from a deep sleep. The man at the desk spoke, using the same words, 'Allo, your friend is downstairs.' He still felt slightly dazed.

There she was, in the lounge. She sat with her student file on her lap, looking healthy and warm. She had to pretend to her parents she was going to her university classes – instead she came to him. Briefly he thought: she will get found out. She smiled at him.

'We can have breakfast here together.' Again, they swung into their own world where it seemed impossible anyone could intervene, it was strong and complete. Yet she had come from a different world to his own; she looked fresh and he felt the opposite.

Quickly he wondered about her parents. They were vague figures in the background to him – he had never met them, even when they had come to England. He had only seen a photograph, back then. In this a thickset Persian man sat stolidly on a chair; he had a fixed, obstinate posture, heavy, as if trying to keep the chair down hard on the ground. His wife sat next to him. She looked incongruous there, sensual, beautiful, in contrast to his large, hulked form. She looked conventional, Shah's wife style. The father looked a man to be reckoned with, fixed in business purposes. He had his fingers in many pies – property building, oil dealing, eyes open for chances.

Three daughters sat beside him, one very young. Zohre herself was looking sideways at her father, slightly nervous, not smiling. The father was rich, saw himself as religious also. He had built and sold houses, blocks in Tehran, his wife's grandfather had been a Persian lord, owning lands. It made only a vague picture. It passed fast through his mind.

He wondered about the home Zohre had come from now, her family house, its atmosphere. It was a zone he was excluded from, in the background as far as he was concerned. Yet it exerted a power he couldn't see in detail. He wasn't going to be invited there. It was separate.

They sat next to each other. She looked at him, laughing, wanting him to be with her in her world. She showed him her books. She was trying to please him, she knew he was interested in these. They drank the tea the man brought, ate the breakfast. The tea came dark, in small glasses, smooth.

'We will visit some friends – first my girlfriend.'

The taxi set off. The city closed round, oppressive. His awareness of it hung back his connexion; he was worried it impeded them. He felt so far uneasy most of the time in the streets; he concealed this. He knew, rationally, there was no point in being disturbed by the city, that it wouldn't help to dislike it. But his whole self seemed set against it. The place was unpleasant, its essence felt part rotten, corrupt. There were more soldiers about today, armed police in shades. She saw him looking.

'Yes, it's soon the day to celebrate the White Revolution. They take care for that.' She didn't want to focus on it. She pointed to walls where posters of the Shah were stuck up prominently with paragraphs in his praise below.

The car pulled up in a side street outside a long tall wall. Trees stuck up behind, elegant and a small stream ran at the edge of the road. Here was quiet. Trees also stood along a deep ditch opposite where water ran fast. The trees were coated in white dust. Zohre told him to wait in the car while she fetched her friend. He heard the girls talking at a distance in the flowing Persian he liked very much to hear, though he didn't understand. Then a girl got in breathlessly. She shook his hand, now rather formal.

'Hello, I am pleased to meet you. I have heard all about you.' Zohre had also squashed in. There seemed something guarded about her friend. She wasn't like the other friends he'd met at the Iran America Society. She was older, more reserved, wary.

'I cannot stay long. I have to go back to work. But I wanted to meet you.'

'She works in a school and a Government office.' Zohre was explaining. Her friend was opening the car door.

'I will see you again – tonight. Now goodbye.'

The woman moved away, back towards an ornate gate in the wall, heavy, and expensive. It swung open electrically and she vanished inside. Now he wondered why they had sat in the taxi to speak and not stood in the road. It was clandestine, the other way. Zohre was talking. 'It's a girls' school. Men aren't allowed inside the grounds. So she had to come out. And it would be frowned on, meeting a man.' She paused, then went on.

'That was Sudabeh – now we'll go to her boyfriend's office. She'll come with us tonight.'

The taxi moved on through blocked streets. He never knew where he was going, Zohre just took him. Now they stopped outside an office block. They went up in a lift a few floors. It was an architects' office. A man in a leather coat and dark glasses come forward, amiable, warm.

'We knew you were coming.' The room was untidy, pleasant – there were architects' drawing boards all around, easels hung with plans. Zohre was explaining how Sudabeh would come later. Another man came to shake hands, the brother of the first.

'Last year – I was in England – studying architecture.'

The atmosphere was loose, welcoming. Zohre was making jokes. An assistant was sent out, laughingly, to get cakes. No-one seemed to mind suspending work for the day, maybe there wasn't much work to be done. Outside the city looked more manageable, seen through wide glass windows from high up; you looked down on roofs, the streets themselves were concealed.

'What do you think of the city?' Ali was curious.

'It seems crowded.' They were laughing, amused.

'Tomorrow', Zohre was saying, 'Ali will take us to your new flat.' The man was grinning.

'You'll like it there. And maybe Sudabeh will come with us too.' Another man emerged from a room.

'She won't come. Her parents won't let her!' Ali turned amused.

'This is Sayd, another brother.' Sayd approached the guest, shook hands.

'And – you know –', he turned to the guest, 'if Sudabeh goes with Ali in his car, he has to drop her round the corner from her parents' place. They mustn't know she's been with him. She has to make something up, late working, out with a girl friend, isn't that right Zohre?'

Zohre was looking back, she didn't look pleased. 'I suppose it is true!' Then she smiled. She didn't her visitor to think she was constrained. She was proud. She wouldn't consciously talk of these things.

Ali was grinning, moving freely to sit on a drawing table.

'My brother – he was in prison. He was a teacher. Now he cannot work again. He can't go abroad, they have taken his passport.' He flung his arm out to show his brother.

'Yes, I told my class about Tolstoy. We read his essays. And the King couldn't allow this. The great King – he is afraid of Tolstoy!' The men were glad to inform the guest of these things.

'And Iranian girls! What do you think of them?' The first brother was asking.

'They tell the truth.'

'Maybe – sometimes.' The men were laughing. There came the sound of a bell. Zohre was smiling, but she looked at the foreign man wanting to be reassured – she didn't want things put in any negative light. She didn't like jokes about women. She knew the social things were true, there were imprisonings, restrictions, but she didn't want to dwell on them. You could waste your energy. 'It'll be Sudabeh', she told them.

*

Sudabeh came in, joking. 'Well, Ali, how are your other girlfriends?' She looked at him challenging, wanting him to tease her back. He shrugged, grinning again.

'And your other boyfriends?' The woman smiled, and turned to the guest.

'I'm really glad to see you again.' She was warm this time. She turned back to Ali. 'So now we can all go to eat.' The other brothers sat grinning at the drawing tables, lazily, amused at the new arrival. They'd stay in the office.

Outside it was dark. Big trees grew alongside the ditch at the edge of the pavement. A few people walked quickly along in the icy air. They crossed a wide road and walked to a parked car. The two couples set off together for a restaurant near the hotel.

In the car he looked out again at the streets and Zohre sat leaning against him. It was all better, the darkness hid the shops and offices, there were fewer people about. The car moved down the highway and the man felt a sudden pleasure, a sense of achievement. He was here, after all, so far from England with her. The girl drew him towards her, this was the foundation. She had caused him to be here. The city, horrible in the intense daylight, receded. The car was warm. Ali and Sudabeh sat in the front, relaxed; a physical ease filled the car. The wipers cleared off snow that had begun to fall.

Outside the hotel Ali parked the car, backing it up to a frozen heap of snow in the gutter, about three feet high. The icy surface glittered under the yellow street lights. They got out into the cold and walked to a restaurant nearby.

A waiter in a black dinner jacket showed them downstairs into a large dark room. Zohre was looking at her watch. She took the visitor's hand at the table.

'I must be home at half past seven.'

Sudabeh agreed.

'So must I.'

It gave them all a couple of hours. Both women accepted they couldn't be late. They were agitated at the thought of worrying their parents, having questions asked if they were later.

They sat, talking. All was relaxed, they spoke of nothing in particular. Zohre was enjoying being herself with the man, it was more like the mood of the English evenings, they drifted off into a warm, separate space. She liked touching him as she explained the food. Sudabeh and Ali were talking, they'd known each other a long time, they might be married, Zohre had said. But Sudabeh sometimes saw a much older man, maybe even a minister, Zohre wasn't sure, went for lunch with him. There were some tensions for this. But tonight things went easily along.

The two girls left after eating one course, leaving the two men alone together. Ali accepted the departure humorously, as a usual event.

'Why must they go now?'

'For their parents – otherwise their parents would be angry.' Ali was easy, used to negotiating the circumstance. The foreign man wondered what form the anger could take to be so effective a constraint. It was hard to accept the conditions as fair, understand why they seemed general. He felt alien, unfamiliar.

They were talking.

'Yes, my brother was in prison. He taught a forbidden book. And tomorrow is Shah's Day – to celebrate the king. No-one much likes him now.'

'What would they like?'

Ali shrugged. 'They don't know. Maybe something worse comes. We seem unlucky that way. Who knows what happens?' He seemed gloomy, lit a cigarette. There was a pause, then Ali continued.

'And you'll be married? I can help you, these Iranian fathers.' Now Ali was grinning. 'And you'll come to my house. I'll introduce you to some people.'

'Yeah, that will be good. What about Zohre? Can she come too?'

Ali looked regretful. 'You know, her parents wouldn't let

her. If she was married, yes, she could come. And now, her parents wouldn't like it.'

'But the girls miss out.'

'Yes, it's true. The girls miss out. They can talk to their girlfriends, that's allowed.'

Ali walked with him to the hotel. The courtesy pleased the guest. It showed concern, friendship and he was glad to have that. They were away from the English assumption that everyone can manage his own affairs and wants no help from anyone else.

'Tomorrow, I will take you and Zohre to your new flat.' He was gone, in the dark and ice. The taillights of his Peugeot 501 swung invisible as the car turned left, was gone into the traffic.

Back in his room the Englishman was thinking. Ali had told him some new things. There could be no public criticism of the King or Iranian society. Those who made such criticisms or were suspected of them would be imprisoned, or shot, tortured perhaps. Others, like Sayd, the brother, had passports removed, could not go abroad to work, and were forbidden to work in Iran. English and American governments gave support to such procedures. They sold military equipment and training services to the regime. England had also received billions of pounds as a loan from Iran during its time of economic supervision by the international monetary fund, a period of cuts. Foreign businessmen made no criticisms of the Shah so long as they profited. Where money making was concerned, nothing else counted. Meanwhile, in England, the government would pose as just and righteous, see itself, London, as superior zones.

He was sickened; there, outside the window the city was just nothing at all, a pointless assembly where money was made and some people grew rich as others worked for them, instruments. The basis was the same as in England. He was glancing at two Iranian newspapers he had picked up in the hotel lobby. One carried comments in English about the

Shah's achievements and aims. He wanted to build a new, superior civilisation based on material development to rival Europe. The paper carried columns of praise in which English and American firms, with others from Japan, Germany, elsewhere in Europe, declared their support for the King in lavish terms. A member of the BP group of companies 'had the honour' to express its 'sincerest congratulations to the Shah'. RCA had seen fit to praise the 'wise leadership' of 'his imperial majesty'. Rockwell International expressed pride in 'implementing the principles of the White Revolution'. The men who had placed these statements in the paper had perhaps known of the regime's repressive forms. Yet they had simply gone ahead. If money was to be got by endorsing the King's methods anyway, they would endorse them. It was the sellers' way. Maybe they agreed with the King's methods, who knew.

He remembered, back in England, he'd read a political leaflet, without much interest, about Iran. It had referred bizarrely to certain Moslem clergymen the Shah had attempted to restrain. The suggestion was that if the Moslem clergymen were allowed more freedom to make critiques and apply more human values then Iran would at once become a more equable and just society. English people were invited to write to their MPs about the clergymen and their plight. The Shah's spy and torture networks, his waste of money on military projects would be eliminated if the clergy had more influence. It seemed like rubbish. How could a bunch of clergymen affect a change? Meanwhile the Shah's oppressions continued.

What did it have to do with Zohre and himself? They should move on, as themselves, get out of these contexts. He lay on the bed, sleep came fast.

'Rolls Royce – who gives a fuck? Everyone thinks they make cars, not weapons.' The English men were standing in London in the grounds of a palace. A few red buses passed, boring, beyond glossy black railings.

'We sell the Shah the weapons. It's billions for us. We don't give a fuck either.' He was emphatic. 'And who knows, here, what goes on there?' The two men were discussing. A bent official was beckoning them forward, like a bouncer in an expensive suit, and they went in a little slit door at the palace side. Inside a fattish man with pouchy cheeks waited, irritable. He began at once.

'So, I go across and the deal is done?' He was aloof.

A minister was speaking back, and Henley was behind, chief seller. 'You just show up, that's all.'

'In my role as envoy for trade?'

'Naturally, what else?'

The fat man prince was gazing. Of course it would be done. The ministers and businessmen knew it, he had known it all along, he'd go to the pre-celebration, White Revolution, seal the deal. There'd be Persian tarts, maybe underage, and food. It was rumoured the King would later be spending billions to entertain heads of State, his mother maybe, and their families. It would be a kick arse day like when somewhere else he'd been allowed to machine gun near convicts out on exercise from his helicopter in Arabia under supervision. And billions for an English company! Henley had represented the issues, there'd be tax revenue too. He couldn't care, that was pissy talk, Henley bored him.

The Ministers and Henley were buttoning up tight coats, there'd be cameras at the gates, they'd announce the deal. What you might get, flesh sliced off at the knees, chests torn with metal holes, wasn't a concern. It was the selling that counted. The Prince was pissing in his privy, upper loops, and the two men were thinking of doing the same as they saw crowds outside the palace gates, piss on them. It would never be explained what they really did, the élite, you had to be in it to know. As it was they explained as little as possible, to run on as untouchable was the aim. And people liked this, made no challenge, easy times. The sellers, the highest ones, were the people to be, and those in their closest circles. All was run by the sellers and the aim was to make this even more, unshakeably, the case as the future became present, to screw all down as a world owned and run by sellers and money alone. The richest sold, Henley sold arms.

A few days before they'd been in the country house, a security service residence.

'It's for selling.' A tall thin man was pointing to a tube with fins, on a stand. Behind, a fire burned in a wide fireplace and men stood in a small group. The scientist was explaining, it was weaponry, a British tank fired it.

'Or a larger model, fired from a base unit with warhead.' Henley was smiling. 'They'll buy it and have a war. Then we sell more. Everyone gains. Looks small though, don't it?'

'Blah-ha' A kind of laugh went up as Henley, an intellectual among them, was pretending to draw and fire. The Prime Minister was laughing, loaded and mock fired back. It was like school days.

The conversation was fading, the deal was done, you flew out to finalise. Henley was talking. The other minister looked bored but Henley was pressing on, with product information.

'Look, the warhead has blades of metal that fly out and cut people to sections. And they're working in the US on a bit that extends and bores through concrete like a mad independent machine drill and squirts explosive into holes.'

Henley went with the products. He was a coming man, more popular with the people than the Prime Minister, even tipped to supersede. He talked more.

'We need to root out those against. Take the Moslem clergymen. They're shits. Islam's shit. We get those missiles out to the Persian King, wings of the dove style, quiety quiet, on the creep. He pays, every time. He can turn them too on his neighbours. We'll show him how.' The others let him talk, agreed, the power was with him, he was on the rise. 'So it's operation Fuckabilly.' His voice was rising, he could inspire.

Hands were shaken. No-one much liked each other here. Splitting off back to separate identities was the mode. Insect breath was breathed, bodies moved as the neurons twitched across brains, there was motor co-ordinating, chemical machines. A queer juice ran in the flesh, there were tubes of blood, the missiles would break other people open, tear bodies into flitches like with Christmas hams.

Henley was on again.

'Millions on development – those weapons! We get it back. The Persian King buys them up. We keep him in power – it's economic fuckabilly. And on and on! The loans he's giving! Maybe they won't be repaid, too!'

The ministers were out of the door, the scientist was with them, there were men down from Derby, Rolls Royce, also Dowty men, GCHQ from Gloucestershire. The sale was in the bag. They'd go to Piccadilly and talk anti-subversion, keep up the canon of selling and elsewhere the blood would blow out of veins, there'd be the twisted formats of body systems broken open on the ground and money in the Exchequer and private company accounts, nationalised armaments companies too, boosts for the English. They'd sit for a meal, all out of contact, then there'd be the team to Tehran, missiles and other weapons already en route by ship. Some were flown out, RAF near Oxford they go from, Brize for the early flight out. Henley was gobby, boring, fuckabilly days.

There were the soldiers in the deal, training providers – the bus was already bumping on an unmade-up road, half dark. You flew out from Brize to an airstrip in Iran and it was training, you'd be showing how. The officer had told them. They looked thick, sub-intelligent. A kind of gallows was at an entrance to a yard where a man was spinning rigid, feet off ground.

'They don't mess around here.' A man in British army clothes was laughing, his square face with short hair had eyes set back in rectangle slots, heart beat steady, life was in him, a low throb of being. The lads were grinning, they would train foreigners, it was easy meat. British trainers were preferred and the Government sent them, it was bridging cultures and the training went with the weapons sales. The code word was fuckabilly and now they were swarming off the Persian bus.

In the distance mountains loomed.

'Christ, we're a long way off here'. A gale of laughing went up and the Captain had come to meet them, they were alert, not at ease, saluting like wound up dolls.

'Straight at them.' The Captain was pointing down in the part dark to where bundles were strapped to hurdle jumps like at Cheltenham races. Running in from the sides too came the foreign troops, for the training.

'Show them how it's done, British Boys', the Captain was shouting.

The men ran in a dwindling geometric pattern towards the sacks and Persian troops were mixing in. 'Have at them' the Captain was calling and they were heaving at the sacks with bayonets, pressing in on soft contents. It was dark, all felt velvety and slick.

'Fuck on lads, strike and jab, you're on the job don't be a sap'. It was the regimental slang chant, foxtrot days back in the 20s and the Captain was calling. The foreign Persian troops were pressing boots on the sacks, kicking out. A kind of ooze, sensed not seen, was on the grass and some sacks were vaguely splitting.

'Fucking hell, it's the real thing.' A kind of lust was up in the British boys. Now a new voice was calling.

'These are insurgents, like those at home who block the path to your land's supremacy.'

A foreign accent was sharp, there were words in a queer foreign voice, the sacks were splitting more and it was manly horseplay, body parts flew about the jump and the Captain was laughing. One sack was twitching. He put his finger to his lips.

The men stopped in mid horseplay, to watch. A faint smile was on their faces like at the Christmas officers' mess pantomime. They watched then their officers perform. There were moonings, fake shags; one officer mimed a dark person having a torture hood put over his head. Now the Captain tiptoed up to the sack, took a spade from the jump. Then with a huge soggy crack the spade's steel blade smacked the sack at its bulge. There was a small whimper and a dark seep visible in the black was running. The Captain stood back.

'Helping to clear the land here of subversives.'

One of the training party had raised his hand.

'Is it an atrocity sir?' He was laughing.

'Yes, it's an atrocity.' The Captain's voice was raising. 'And here's to bloody more of them.'

The men were calling out, as if at a toast. The foreign troops were in a cluster, watching on.

Sayd was out, he went walking. His school was far out in the countryside. He could see a knot of men below, from a slight rise. Then he was sliding down a path. Through the thin branches of a bush he could see blood seep from a sack. He was watching, fixed.

Someone was creeping, he was caught up.

'A fucking watcher boy', there was calling out. It was fast, no-one spoke, he was thrown in a van by two Persian soldiers, he was a no-one, there by chance, maybe, but they'd put him in prison anyway.

'Fucking looking.' The English soldier couldn't get over it, as if someone had been observed at intimate washing, and a dirty looker too, maybe a pervert type used to spying in. Or, worse, maybe a type against order, an organizer. The van took him away.

The Captain was speaking on. He would intensify morale. 'This is our training field. Shit to the subversive Moslem. The Communist terror boys.' The officer was exclaiming, egging on.

A kind of tumult was rising. It had been a success. A few were pissing on the sacks, Persian trainees also.

'Remember lads. Just now the IMF are running England. By being here we are helping the economy. Our deal goes with the weapons deal. The King here has loaned our government millions. He has paid millions for weapons and services.' The Captain believed in truth and educating his men.

A soldier had his hand up.

'What's IMF?'

'That's International Monetary Fund to you laddie.' Some Americans who'd drifted in, stood casual, laughed.

The troops were sniggering, it was a fuck, they didn't know where they were, there were laughs, what does 'monetree' mean, but they'd killed militants, it had been a good day. The foreigners were looking on, some were tentatively spading sacks, finishing off. And back at Brize was the network, the missiles would be in soon, the Captain knew. Henley was fixer, he'd soon be high in politics too, was the rumour. Strong leaders were best, the coming man.

The Englishman woke up early. Today he'd be leaving for the flat. He knew Zohre would come soon. The phone rang, as usual. He went and sat with her in the lounge, drinking tea.

'The old women who saw us here before, she asked me when I was going to be married.' The girl smiled with a kind of pride.

'What did you say?'

'I didn't tell her anything.'

It was the first time either of them had mentioned marriage since he had come. This woman, could she be his wife? Could he be her husband? She sat next to him – he was filled with desire for her. She kissed him warmly, pulling his face to hers, her hand gentle on his neck. What were her thoughts? She seemed inaccessible partly. He couldn't yet map out for himself her daily life. Her studies at the university didn't seem to mean that much to her. The home with her parents – what was she there? That centre of her life was a mystery to him. She didn't speak about it or discuss it. She drew him to her definitely, he desired her with an energy that amazed him. Yet there was some mystery, something hidden.

Ali appeared suddenly, round the corner of the entrance. They were waiting for him. Zohre went off to pay the hotel bill. The guest watched her hand over the notes, heard her speaking in Persian. She would pay out of her own money because she wanted to. He had little money. But they had decided before he came this didn't matter. But it bothered him. Outside the traffic was building up in the street, light snow had fallen, there was a rattle of tyre chains. It was out there he'd find the job. She'd got plans, they'd go to see people, ask at institutes. Then, she said, he would be paying for her from his salary. She was joking, she'd work too. But it was out in the city – he'd be dependent on what was out there.

They all got in the car, smiling together.

'Let's go – it's in part of the city I've rarely been.' Zohre was enjoying herself. So far all her plans were working out.

The car moved off, weaving into the traffic. They sat jammed up in the lines of cars, smoking cigarettes, talking, waiting for the cars to move. It was their own world in there. Today the traffic was worse than usual. Several main streets were closed because of the festival in honour of the King, White Revolution. Police cars with red lights on top moved along blocked roads passing in and out of the queue. There were armed soldiers at one end of a boulevard, a small line of tanks, made in England, missiles on trucks, the same. There'd be a small parade, a larger one had happened a month earlier. The English queen would perhaps sit later with the Shah to watch the English and American weaponry go by.

'The King is afraid to leave his palace. They will march past a picture instead.' Ali held up his hands in scorn. 'The King of Kings cannot come outside in his own country.' Zohre didn't join in the remarks, much.

'How can anything be changed?' She was gloomy, sharp.

Ali shrugged. 'It's true – could be even worse, next time.'

Zohre sat in a separate mood, looking out of the window, then occasionally joking in Persian or pointing something out. She was excited, a new phase was beginning for her now. She enjoyed the arranging. She wanted the man to be happy, comfortable, with her. Also she was nervous – what if her parents found out before she wanted them to? There were spies, ordinary people, family friends, who would be pleased to gain favour with her father by reporting information to him about his daughters. Yet she didn't entirely believe anyone would tell any tales about her. And how would they know? She was also worried she wouldn't be enough for this man. She wanted him to like the city, the country itself. She didn't want negatives, like the King, made too prominent just yet.

The car turned down street after street. The streets got narrower, maze like. Ali was humorous, asking directions. Labourers waved him further on. There were small shops, bakers with the red fires blasting inside, builders' yards. They turned left into a narrow street where a high rusty sign in the shape of a fish hung heavily above a corner shop. Small terraces of apartments lined the road, three or four storeys high. In many each storey was arranged at a different angle on top of the one below, so odd overhangs were created. The designs of each storey were separate, had been added as extensions over time. Sometimes they collapsed. The narrow street was a cul de sac. To approach it they'd passed mechanics' yards; groups of men stood bending over cars with bonnets up, holding spanners and other tools. Cans of petrol were stacked up in rusty barrels in piles at the back of the yards.

A young couple showed them round. He would have two old rooms attached to their apartment, his own entrance. The television was on in their lounge. The military parade was heading down a city street. There were squads of soldiers, schoolchildren marching. Crowds lined the streets to watch.

Ali was scornful.

'The crowds have been forced to attend.'

No-one in the room showed any interest in the celebration, the attitude was derision. The King had blown his chance, there was no respect. The guest was left by the television. Zohre had gone with the other woman to check his rooms over. He could hear her voice rise and fall close by, in the rhythmic intonation he liked. Ali was also there. Everyone was being kind. How would it be, working in this city?

He was shown round the small flat. He would have his own entrance at the back of the house. There was one room and then as well a bathroom, in a corridor. Thick green curtains hung down the height of the room at the far end, covering long glass windows. A door opened out onto a small tiled verandah with a small yard just below. In the middle a fountain was wrapped up in a thick sheet of polythene to protect it from damage in the winter cold. Surrounding the whole yard was a high green metal fence rising above a wall, about fifteen feet tall, solid. This was to protect the apartment from thieves. The place was makeshift but he was glad to have it, a refuge.

Inside the room was warm, with an oil stove that heated it well. A tank for oil was next to the cupboard-like bathroom in a dark corridor. Zohre sat now at a small table, looking pleased. All her efforts had come to this result now. She had achieved this. It was their context to begin from. From here they'd go, approach institutes for jobs. It would be a practical base. Also she would come here, before or after the classes at the university. It was a contrast to her own home.

Back in the room she had unpacked his case. It was nearly five o'clock and dark outside.

'I must go soon.' Zohre was checking her watch. He was getting used to her early departures. 'Tomorrow I will come early, don't worry.' They were thanking Ali, who got up to leave. He'd give Zohre a lift to a taxi stand. It was time for them to go.

'Do not go out – you will get lost!' Zohre moved to kiss him.

The big green gate in the thief-proof fence banged shut as they went out. He was alone, then, in the unfamiliar land. The atmosphere in the room was heavy, uncreated. They would both together make something here. He had to start everything afresh. He wondered what he should do. There was the bed, the cooking ring, the clothes on a stand. He wondered why she had unpacked his case. She enjoyed doing things for him. He thought of her efforts, her help. He knew the efforts hadn't been easy for her. It was a new venture for her too. What would happen? Things seemed stripped down. You filled them out, bit by bit. She wouldn't tell her parents until he had a job. What kind of job did she imagine he'd get?

She was heading north, to her parents' apartment in a rich, quiet suburb. She had her room, comforts. She was pleased; deceptions were hard and she feared chance spies.

He woke up with the light shining through the curtains. Outside he heard a wailing, a rhythmic chanting that died away suddenly. He got up, curious. No doubt it was a prayer. The sound hung in the room, potent. He washed quickly, expecting the bell to ring at any moment. He was excited again. For the first time since his arrival they would be by themselves in their own room, together. He couldn't even telephone her – she had warned him carefully not to. 'My father must know nothing', she told him. So he was dependent on her coming. He wouldn't know how to find her if she didn't come. He couldn't go to her home. The father loomed up, a presence to be taken account of. He fixed a shape; in England they'd made their own, no-one else was involved.

The bell rang suddenly. He opened the door onto the veranda, went across the small yard where patches of snow were permanently frozen in winter. The outer door opened easily, she was there. She came in, leaning towards him, putting her hand on his shoulder, kissing his cheek. He thought she looked very beautiful with her black hair shining under a small woollen hat, her face glowed healthily in the cold air. He greeted her warmly.

She walked across the yard, slightly ahead of him. He was pleased and easy with her so near. She complemented him in some way he couldn't fathom, set something free in him. She moved unconsciously; she seemed vulnerable, with a physical trust as she entered the flat. She took off her coat and hung it on the stand. The room was warm, the stove hummed. Some books were left open on a table at the far end of the room.

She smiled. 'What did you do last night?' she asked gently. 'Were you all right?' Her tone was soft and teasing, concerned.

'I read, cooked some food.' He looked at her as he replied. The words didn't mean anything much. Their real attention was with each other elsewhere. She laughed, opened her bag.

'I've brought you some more things – from home. My mother will think I eat too much – the things disappear.' She pulled out a tin of cherries, some chocolate and biscuits. She laughed, happy in this new world. The long green curtains covered the windows completely – the room was pleasantly enclosed, secluded. He sat on the bed while she sat at the low table, turning the pages of his books, absently.

Both of them felt shy. She got up suddenly and came to sit on the bed next to him. It was strange to be there together at last. She leaned forward to kiss him. The room was theirs, it was a release. She slid closer to him and he moved his hand across her warm, strong back. She looked at him as she lay there. She wanted to please him. She smiled again with teasing pride. They were close together in the big warm bed. Her body was brown and healthy, vividly alive.

What did she feel? He looked back at her, wondering, knowing he loved her. She lay there in the bed with the sheet wrapped round her. She was very beautiful to him. Questions came vague. What were the constraints of her family life, what customs did she accept? He knew she had been brave to defy the conventions so far. Outside the green curtains the city streets and conditions ran, to take account of, an unease.

She looked at him, her eyes lit up with pleasure and pride. She could help him and love him – it was simple.

'What would our children be like?' She asked suddenly.

'After two years I would like children. All boys.' She spoke as if she had thought about it; she said boys, aiming to please him, a joke but following Persian custom. He realised he would like to have children with her. It was a new desire. He imagined them suddenly, chattering in Persian and English.

'We could be married soon. I can ask my father.' She spoke mischievously, meaning what she said. She didn't explain more. He wondered why her father was the one to decide, was it really that way?

'Yes, we can decide.' He switched it round, maybe on purpose, not thinking much.

He got out of bed, hopping down as it was so high. He would make tea for them both. Zohre lay warm under the thick bedclothes. Her shoulders raised them beautifully, her black hair was splendid, lying shaggily on the white pillow. She lay curled up, on her side, nearly asleep. Why should anyone be in charge of her?

He waited by the cooking ring for the water to boil. There was an old dented pan, without a handle, to heat the water. He liked to squat there almost naked. The old stove kept the room hot. He saw her move under the blankets, look at him sleepily. It was their world again. She freed him with her naturalness. He took her the tea – she stretched out her arm carelessly to take it. He sat on the side of the bed.

'I shall ask my father – yes? And before we will find a job, so we can tell him that. It will be easy, we can go to colleges, ask there.'

He nodded back. A line was set out, how it would be. A kind of control seemed to have been removed and passed on instead to the older man, remote and unseen. He wondered what he was giving away but did it anyway.

She was silent for a moment, then looked at him, kissed him. Things were arranged, she was pleased.

They'd go out, buy some food. Outside it had begun to rain, the polythene covering the fountain in the yard drummed with the drops. The alleyway beyond the security gate wound towards a main road, an old woman bent her head from a window as they came out. Tall buildings along the street looked transient; the zone was makeshift, buildings had no root, could be knocked down, replaced. Sometimes the King did that, wiped out an area, redevelopment or reprisals. Her father did demolitions, was a builder also. The rain fell heavily, dust was streaked then ran off cars and buildings. Big gullies at the edge of the pavement carried swirling water and rubbish along the street. Army officers in braid caps and dark glasses moved among women in black veils.

They went into a small shop like a cupboard in a wall, bought meat and then tea, choosing leaves from a sack. Zohre also picked up a loaf of solid sugar. 'We can chip bits off, for the tea.' She liked it, practising to be a wife.

Back in the room she sat on the bed pulling off her soaking shoes. Her hair was curled with the rain where it was uncovered by her hat. She shook her head to get rid of the water. He looked at her – she corresponded to himself. Without her he couldn't progress. It was essential for her to be there. He knew she would have to go home soon, for her parents. The green curtains were pulled across the tall windows. In the evening it grew cold very fast. He opened the door to go out onto the veranda to fetch milk he kept out there. It was black outside. He saw the stars vivid and clear above. The red light of a plane flashed overhead, come from another place.

She looked at him closely, smiling as he came back in. She was cutting up some cake.

'I would like to stay here with you, live here.' She was questioning even as she laughed – did he want her? The room was dark, with just a small lamp casting a circle of light on the table. He went across to her.

'I want you to stay here, too.' They both knew she couldn't stay, she would have to obey her parents and go home.

'When we are married I'll be here all the time.' She was pleased, as she spoke; things would go well, she was sure of it.

She changed the subject, laughing. 'You have learned some Persian. I'll teach you some words. Here, what's this?' She pushed the ashtray gently forwards. Her hair brushed his face as she bent near him. He sat on the bed next to him. She held the ashtray in her hand, moved closer. 'What is it called? I taught you yesterday.' They lay back on the bed, crushing his grammar books. She looked at him, shy, her eyes lit up in question. They lay together for a long time with the rain falling outside. It was very peaceful, there together. The city felt far off.

'I must go soon', she told him. He didn't want her to leave. He felt deserted as she put on her coat and her small hat, still wet. The door clicked shut as she went out into the alley. He wondered what she thought about on the pavement, waiting for the taxi to go home. Things were set out, into the future.

The Englishman woke up, heard the prayer as usual hang in the air. The rhythmic, committed tone attracted him. Today, he knew, she had the plan to push on with – he had to have a job before she told her father anything.

She rang the bell. They went out, together again, through the blocked streets that were demoralising and blank. Dusty shop fronts, imitating boutiques in London, lined the pavements like guards. Today she seemed subdued, something was on her mind. 'My parents must know soon – and I have a headache.' She smiled at him, took his hand. The taxi was stopping below a concrete flyover that ran level with the second storey of a line of shops and offices, built box-like out of more concrete. The air was heavy with fumes from the upper and lower roadways, cars moved past noisily.

Behind tall railings lay a group of barrack-like buildings. Armed guards stood as usual at an entrance: one, legs apart was on a low roof, a machine gun across his chest. Zohre had rung through, there was a possibility to work here, at the institute. They waited in an annexe where an old woman dozed in a chair. She woke up, offered them tea. They would have to wait. Zohre was chatting to the woman, friendly.

The inner door opened, a man came in, Persian, pushing through suddenly. He wore a brightly coloured check coat, half-length, with a zip up the front. His hair was black and curled and he had a small beard, wore shades.

'What can I do for you then?' There was a slight U.S. drawl.

It was explained, the need for a job, qualifications presented. The Iranian was impressed, took a quick liking to the couple.

'You're here because of her, of course? You have to watch the fathers here. Isn't that right?' He turned to the girl, who stayed non-committal. Then he swung back to the man.

'You know about the universities here?' His tone changed, became scornful. 'You can't say what you want. I will go out, to America. I have to work here – five years. That's the rule. Then I'll leave. You can say anything in America. And the women understand sex.'

Zohre was talking back in Persian. He turned to the man again. 'We all have to watch our fathers, bosses. So I will speak for you, to the director. It will take a little time, but it will be all right. I've read your resumé. We need someone like you. You'll need a work permit. Good luck you two. Look out for the fathers!' He was gone, calling out, off to teach a class, maybe, or simply off.

Zohre was cheered up, happy. 'You won't have time for me when you work.' She was joking. 'But you can take me to a restaurant with your first salary.' Still, things weren't entirely secure, fixed.

They'd meet Sudabeh, who worked close by. They'd have to walk a short distance. The air was oppressive and dusty, though sun shone. A few trees stood at intervals in a side street along the edge of a deep gulley, like a stream that ran parallel to the roadway. He waited outside a building with a high wall, out of place, slightly forlorn. Zohre had gone inside to collect her friend. Only women worked here and were allowed in. The city felt strange, he was cut off with Zohre inside. The two girls came out, they walked to a café. He was walking unstably, breathing thin air; the street landscape glittered unreal in the sun.

They sat at a dark table. Sudabeh was dressed smartly, more formal than Zohre's other friends, finished off. She seemed different, not with Ali. Suddenly a tall older man was looming at the table, addressing the woman, urbane. There was a slight scent about him. Sudabeh stood up, explained she'd sit briefly at his table.

Zohre was explaining to the man. 'Her parents want her to marry him. But she likes Ali more. She has to be polite.'

'Who is he?'

'He works in a ministry. But also he has his own businesses, he is rich.'

They glanced across, the man was talking smoothly, quiet. Sudabeh was getting up to leave. They walked with her to the high wall, then back to outside the institute.

They stood outside, below the flyover again. It was raining now, the air was loaded with car fumes, hard and wet to breathe. Again they flagged taxis down. None stopped. Then a pick up truck pulled over. They were quiet now, inside the cab. Zohre had fulfilled a duty, the truck drove through the rainy, choked streets.

He wanted to tell her what he was thinking, how he'd felt when she'd gone to fetch Sudabeh. He was dependent on her here. For some reason it wasn't possible to speak naturally. Anyway, what did his awarenesses signify? He was sick of them. What good was it, his repetitive feeling that the city always struck him as strange, disturbing? At the same time Zohre was what he wanted.

They turned to stop at a kerb. They'd go into another café. The movement towards a job had definitely begun, it was her plan. In his mind was the tall, older man bending over Sudabeh and talking to her in hushed, persuading tones, a shadow image, the ministry, rich businesses, Sudabeh's parents pushing her.

Now for Zohre a kind of stress ran in her that these work things should be completed, it would go well with her father then. She could tell her parents when he had a job. Now she smiled at him, touched him lightly under the table, discreet. She had another plan for the afternoon.

The Prince and envoy had been taken through, he was royal, it was what happened to him. He had a sort of function, was paid for it, now he was here. Now, inside a great hall he'd be escorted further in. Outside a wide spread of asphalt led through trees to a high wall. The grounds were all enclosed. Wires ran across and there was a tower the foreign King had built to celebrate his kingdom, outside the wall. It was queer, foreign, a meaningless shape, costly to construct, empty, modern.

Now he was in, there was a glass-topped table with fruit on and light stands set with jewels that glittered. It was getting dark.

'Two kings.' A man was holding a hand to be shaken.

'No, it's my relatives. Not me. Of course, I might succeed.'

'Yes, but for this evening we are two. And later this month the rest of your family will come from London. For the celebrations. The Empress expects them, too.'

The room was edgy, something latent. The two kings sat on high chairs, made of oak, costlier versions of those in an English bourgeois home, such as a minister or finance man might inhabit. The King was squinting at the second king. His eyes had a detached high look. He was pouring from a decanter that glistened with gold leaf.

'We are kings. We can do as we like.' He pointed suddenly to a queer bundle of clothes that was beginning to stir in the corner of the room. All was half-dark. It seemed a leg was coming out. A bent figure was then still, an old woman's face poked from cloth surrounds.

THE PERSIAN WEDDING

'A leper – a dirty leper! My police pick them up from the streets. Tonight I have brought one here to show.' The second king was cottoning on, there'd be a display, something royal. It was good to feel the restraints lifting, a deep licence start. The King was up, casual, reaching for a short plank that lay against his chair. The old woman was bent, there were the knotted hands, blotches of growths and the king smacked the plank flat across the back of her head. There was a kind of cry and faint spots of red.

He was passing the plank across, to the English visitor, 'Come, try.' The mood was rising, it was breaching. Now the plank came down flatter and harder, the second king was panting, slightly fat. His buttocks bulged like big balls enclosed in his grey flannel trousers. Now the leper was down, he saw her with her arm fixed rigid encrusted with scabs. The plank broke the bone then bounced hard on the top of her head, breaking in the skull membrane. The old woman lay still.

The King was speaking. 'It is good, to do these things. And she was no good, a thief and ill.' The visitor was grinning. It was good to cross boundaries and be royal to an extreme extent.

'We will buy your weapons. And now we will have another guest.'

The second king was looking, there'd be a pause and they'd have more drinks, this time in glasses that were frosted and studded with inset diamonds that caught the light. It was like at home, richer, slightly more vulgar, but they could perhaps be freer here.

'And how is your mother? She will enjoy the visit here next month.'

'Of course. She is well.' He knew she was looking forward to the luxury of the event and it would be a chance to be seen to reinforce economic relations with the emergent land. Also the military appealed to her, the bought tanks and other repressive vehicles would parade, there would be pageants, she'd overlook.

Suddenly the door was flung open. Two guards were dragging a man across the room.

'He is from our prison, here in Tehran, Evin.' The man was lashed up in a heavy cable. He lay in the centre of the room, still, on the polished wooden floor blocks. The second king was looking. Maybe he was a dissident. He himself hated those in England who were against the right and his own modes. A queer mood rose again of being in a new, more advanced state where dealings were clear and a correct strategy was in place. It was royal, like in the past, but made new. He had a vague sense of history, kings had burnt down their enemies' homes, had people stabbed up alleys, done as they wanted. You had girls, you were the master. The man was gurgling on the ground, he'd wrenched his head round to look at the kings on the chairs.

At once the King was drawing a golden gun from a briefcase. He put it quietly down on the glass-topped table next to the bowl of fruit and the saucers with pistachio nuts in. Some kind of regular routine would take place. The man on the ground was having a semi-convulsion, his head was twitching in the cables and there was blood coming from his mouth where he had bitten part through his tongue.

'They give him medicine in the prison.' The King was squinting, touching the arm of his guest. 'Sometimes it takes them like that.'

His eyes were half closing, he crossed his thin, spare legs, his face hung with lips sharp like razor blades, he seemed to be rising. The second king watched the first, the Persian wore a cream suit and highly polished brown shoes, his face was etched with strict order.

'Fucking reptile shits!' The fatter guest was up, shouting at the bound man. He went over and kicked him clear in the face. He had on shoes based on a military design, heavy, that he had made in London, respectable. Now the man's nose and eye hung crooked, blood crept out.

'Yes, he is against us. He is against you, too, against the weapons you sell, support you give. He is of the vile.' The

King was speaking softly, his words were creeping like the blood. The second king was over, kicking again, the man was gurgling, there was the gold gun, you picked it up and cracked it off, like in the army, he'd trained as an officer, seen service, the bullets were cracking in. He was panting. The guards stood impassive. Usually it was the King who hit the action; this time the guest had begun.

The King was grinning, a hawk grin, He held himself tight in his chair, tensed up as if he could spring. 'He was a religious shit. He said Islam was against arms. A low, vile, fool.'

A strand of saliva hung unnoticed from the guest's mouth. The King handed a napkin across.

'Such napkins were used to douse Christ's wounds down from the cross. You hate to have royalty and quality contravened. I can sense it in you. You suffer, like your mother, at the sense of it.'

The guest was settling back in his chair, it was like officers after polo. Briefly he was wondering if he had perhaps damaged his watch. It had cost £47,000 and he'd treated himself to it back in London only a week ago. It was well to look a rich part. But the watch luckily seemed to be unharmed. He drifted off into a reverie. Only he went further, there were darker aspects. When he came to a small girl about eight had come in the room and sat straddling the Persian King as he fondled her ever more intimately. He felt his own penis rise as he observed. Then, next to him, a girl of twelve came to stand. He lifted her skirt and was molesting. The two men sat on their chairs, high backed, put the lights out. The King had explained, 'prisoners' children', children of the executed. They were used to it, even had developed a liking for this kind of love. The Empress kept them in her school and nursery for prisoners' children, orphans, good works. A kind of low moaning filled the room, kings' purr.

Zohre had another idea. It had gone well at the institute. Now they would go to another place, ask about work.

'It's a friend of my father's. He's starting up a school. I don't like him, he asked to meet me and my friends. He borrows money from my father. But we can ask.'

It didn't seem a wise plan. But he put the awareness away. They were back again, at the flyover where the traffic hung in the air at two levels; the rain locked the fumes down so you breathed them in. You couldn't think clearly. He accepted what she said as she led here, knew the ways.

The taxi wound them through the jammed streets, across massive, chaotic intersections. A few tanks stood in the road, readying for more celebration. The car stopped in a complex of just and partially built blocks. The Persian script of the road name swam in the rain, snake curves and dots.

She was pulling him by the hand to get out of the rain. She liked to touch him, discreet, in this place. His spirits were suddenly low as if the wrong thing was happening. Why did they need to come here, when the outcome of the morning was looking good? She was worrying, she wanted something fixed, some definite post to tell her parents he had.

The lift vibrated as it passed just finished brick openings up to a completed floor. Zohre pressed the bell. There was a pause and a queer, older man, wizened, opened up. Zohre was speaking the Persian lilt. The master would see them. She was speaking, 'It's his servant, an old uncle.' The withered man seemed more scared. There were bruises across his cheek. All around was incomplete, wires stuck out of brick, there were crates with school materials in, books, desks.

A door swung open and a tall man moved forward, uncertain at once to see the girl and the foreigner. He knew her, she was the daughter of his friend, Mr Ghani. He shut it back, how he'd asked her, when her father was out of the room, to go to a club with him, bring her friends. Now he was in debt, here, there, to her father most. He would rise up, to the high circle, the school would be just part of his system of enterprises, he'd have a chain. He was smiling, she had told him her friend was coming, from England.

The room was fitted out, weird, there was a desk and high backed chair, behind on the wall a picture of an old scene from Europe, a waterfall, a mountain with snow, mediocre. There were arm chairs like in an old style Headmaster's study in England, but on a Persian carpet. He was bending forward, his eyes bulging.

'You could make us tea, Zohre. While we talk.'

'Yes, and I could work here too. I could teach some things.'

'Perhaps as a secretary only.' He was dismissing her. He turned to the foreign man.

'You see, here is the school. I teach, everything the American way. They repeat, they learn. It will be languages.'

He was looking, taking in Zohre's visitor. In his mind a dilemma was shaping up. Thoughts ran fast. Did her father know this man was here? And how should he, the father's friend, behave? Perhaps he should report back the news of the man's arrival, what she did with him. After all, he needed loans, had to repay debt. What if the father found out he had known and not told?

'Yes, yes, you could teach here. You have PhD. It would be easy for you. They repeat, you speak. That way they learn fast. And you can use a book too. Many of them girls, all very nice.' He was grinning, carried away, Zohre dancing at a night club, her friends in short skirts, you drew closer. Or maybe you just lunged, half forced, he'd done that, you could get away with it, some girls didn't care. Here, in his office, prostitutes could come. But they'd be dirty girls. He drew himself up.

'And, yes, with Zohre's father. I can speak for you. I am sure he will agree. I can help.' He was passing down from the desk, a box of cigarettes.

'I can teach here, why not?'

'Yes, yes, it's settled. Of course part-time at first.'

A queer silence filled the room. Everything was wrong, the foreign man had no trust in the situation. Zohre was coming in with the tea. She had been waiting outside until the men had finished their business, she knew the expected protocol. The man turned to her.

'Well, well – so this is your fiancé?' She looked back at him, not really thinking, in some kind of separate mode. She dreamed things out, moved them on if they made her uneasy. 'Yes, it is', she was replying without thinking. To her the man was low, not really a family friend, he came for money, to make a connection. And perhaps her father used him in some suspect way, got him to do jobs or tasks. She knew very little about what her father did, how high he reached. Just now she wanted things fixed, to be married.

Or maybe she had, through stress, deliberately brought him here. The Englishman was thinking. This Persian man is sure to tell her father; he could tell him anytime, this evening, in a week, before she tells him. Maybe she had miscalculated. Or did she want her father to be told? All was unclear.

They were being shown out. In the lift she kissed him hard on the lips. He knew she hadn't brought him on purpose, an oblique way to let her father know. She had got confused.

It was getting harder to head on. The rain was falling in dark sheets, mixing the snow on the pavements to slush. At the school he wouldn't earn much, maybe not enough to rent a room. A thick swirl of black water was boiling down a drain, she was clutching his arm, a group of military men stood in long, thick coats at a crossroads, white caps on with the jutting, braided wide peaks. A few had the shades still on that ran with rain. Down a side road he saw the gun barrel of a tank poking in the dark, there were the military trucks, sealed doors. Once inside things went on discreet, hidden.

She was looking. She rarely spoke of these things. 'I just want to be happy. I cannot change these things by myself. I'm happy with you, it's my best thing.'

He kissed her in reply, was about to speak. Suddenly the officer was waving them on, other people ran too, there was going to be military action, they were round the corner, away.

'Maybe they will arrest some people. Take them to Evin.'

The taxi twisted back down narrowing streets to where his room was. They were advanced, things were building up. At the corner of the alleyway that lead to his back entry was a phone box. They'd use it, call up the institute, see how things were. A few people were queuing, women swathed up in black, just the eyes showing; they waited in the drizzle.

He liked it there, with her. They were both far off, headed out somewhere different. He was glad he was miles from England, plunged in this unknown, yet they might go back. There was the wood there, the lanes they drove along, something apart. But who knew what was here, what was ahead? There'd be queer places, you could travel, borders with other places, you could easily go across, see other zones, or move south, see the southern coast. He'd seen pictures, queer houses built in cliff rock. It could be a free, open time. Or you could penetrate here, in the capital, go in deep.

She was smiling at him, saw he was thinking. It was odd how they made this world, always apart from a mainstream. It was their turn in the phone box. The number was ringing, he heard the Persian lecturer reply, with an American accent.

'Yeah, yeah, it's fine, you can work here. Pleased to have you. The boss is pleased too. Start in a month.' The receiver was down, they looked at each other, smiled fully. A woman in black began to tap the glass, they should come out if the call was done. They pushed out of the door and Zohre lit the woman up with her smile; the woman grinned back, muttered in Persian. 'She wishes us luck,' things moved on, it would be a basic wage but they could manage.

Now they stood again in the drizzle. Zohre was already late, she'd have to go. She was looking overwhelmed, her plan had shaped up. Now she could tell her father. She'd have to pick a time when he'd be receptive. He was often busy, and when home needed to relax. Then there was the religious day when only holy things were to be focussed on.

The taxi took her back, the wipers moved the heavy rain off the windscreen. They were passing the intersection where the tank was; in the dark she saw shapes lying in the road, some men were being pushed into the back of military vans. The avenues grew more spacious as the taxi ran on further from his room at the centre of the network of alleys – there were luxurious blocks now, villas. Quite near the huge monument the king had built loomed up, queer white straddling legs curved upwards in an empty, high sweep. The legs were made to look like the wound cables of a suspension bridge, layered and jammed together, taut. It was sinews, something tensed that swept up. But it swept up into nothing, a kind of emptiness was all the rich climax. It was the national monument.

She felt alone in the taxi; all the time before she knew the man she had had most of her thoughts alone and even now it was hard to speak them. Now the taxi was slowing, it was a low block of apartments, luxurious, her father owned them, had had them built. She would go in, be pleasing, her home, fixed life.

Sayd was walking in the road. There'd been a murder round here, Sayd was recalling. It was like boxes. Some, like himself, were allowed a larger containment, just his right to work and passport were removed. Others were kept in an open prison. Then it dwindled down, tighter, there were normal prison cells, then hidden ones, smaller, into which you disappeared and your name was officially unknown if anyone came inquiring.

But now they were picking him up. He walked back along a boulevard. Water ran harsh. He'd been to some museum, he liked to see ancient mosaics, exchange grins with girl teachers showing classes round. Time hung heavy, he was interested but it was killing time to go, he knew. A van stopped just ahead. A couple of motor bikes were pulling up and two men were walking alongside him, jeans and jackets, shades.

'Mr Sayd?' They were familiar. 'The prison boy? The man who looked when he shouldn't have a few months ago?' He was walking faster, still they were there. 'We have to check on you. See if you've reformed.' Now they were pulling, and he saw the reinforced van doors ahead were open and a group of policemen were laughing as he was pushed in. A few passers by were hurrying on, you couldn't tell, you could be pulled in, anything could happen, security.

Inside they were beginning, the batons were whirling, over the whole body, it was a drill, harm all over. The face in particular was receiving attention, you pulped up the cheeks and battered round the eyes until there was a mess of wounds. It was a warning. They drummed on him and next to his face on the floor he saw a small plate, vehicle made in England, Coventry, an export date. Construction had built in the drain grill for the blood to run out. From time to time those known to have once transgressed would be brought in, mobile units, and given a reinforcing punishment to remind them they were eternal suspects and were at risk, so would never be exempt from surveillances and warnings. It was reminder sessions, western experts had recommended.

The blood was running across his eyes and he could feel a bone in his arm was cracked. They were rolling him, the van doors were open and he was out, fallen hard onto the surface of the side road. The van was motoring on, he saw it turn, he was half kneeling in the road. Someone had come from a house, was helping him in. He'd got a blanket on. He'd sleep, get home to his brothers and aunt later, he'd had worse in prison. He'd get back home, later, he was used to it, part of life.

Ali had called by. Now the Englishman was going again, with Ali, back to his home. The car swung onto an unmade up road on the edge of the city. A few houses were put up here where the roads made a triangle. There were pine trees, all around flat land scrappy. In the distance, miles off, an oil chimney burned red flares, gas.

Ali was heading down a short path. He'd been warm in the car, easy, they'd smoked cigarettes, spoken of the women, Sudabeh's business man. Now the door swung open, there was an older brother in pyjamas, at an architect's easel. Sayd was coming forward, he moved about the house restless, often carrying a book. A younger woman came forward, an aunt. Everyone was friendly, open.

The television showed, in the large room. It was a quiz show, everyone in evening dress. The aunt was talking.

'It's just rubbish, you can't say anything here.' Sayd was explaining. 'She works on the radio. Yesterday it was a talk on Yeats.'

The girl was smiling, slightly rakish.

'Yeah, we have to keep it inoffensive.'

They'd all studied, been out, architecture in Manchester, the aunt interior design in London. Only Sayd hadn't gone, stayed teaching in the mountains.

He was fingering his face, touching bruises.

'In the van – they did this. Some weeks back. In the English vans.' He waved his bandaged arm at the television. 'We cannot speak of it. But everyone knows.'

The screen was fading into news, the King with royalty

from abroad, a fat prince, the Empress at a nursery school, preparation for the celebration. The images blurred.

The aunt was looking at the guest.

'And how is Zohre? Your fiancée.'

It was weird how the word fiancée was used so much.

'It all depends on her father.'

The aunt was looking hard at him, then oblique, across the room.

'Why didn't she ask him before you came?' There was some criticism implicit.

'She thinks he'll agree.'

Ali was listening. He looked at the aunt.

'Here it's all about fathers. They have control. The King is father.'

The aunt watched the two men, replied.

'All our male relatives are dead. We can do as we want.'

Sayd was muttering, 'the King sacked teachers for teaching about Tolstoy. The great leader disliked it.' He was holding out a book in English of Tolstoy's essays to the guest. 'Have it – using it in class got me arrested.'

There was a warm atmosphere, critical, humorous.

'Do Sudabeh or Zohre ever come here?'

'No.' The aunt was replying. 'Their families wouldn't like it. And besides – the ideas here aren't suitable. Sayd has been in prison. There are three unmarried men here too. There could be a scandal.' She smiled. 'But it would do them good to come.'

The guest sat back. He'd like to be here with Zohre. The place seemed warm, relaxed.

'Yes, when you're married you can come. Then the woman does what her husband says. You want to come, she comes. Some husbands might leave a wife here and go off to nightclubs. There are always girls.' The aunt seemed dismissive.

The older brother at the easel looked up. He was thin, wore glasses, less at ease then Ali.

'A man needs girls, Something to relax with, have fun.'

THE PERSIAN WEDDING

The aunt looked back. 'But maybe we are not relaxing, not fun.' She grinned. 'What is fun in our lives? Anyway, I hate fun. That's all people thought about in London.'

'Didn't you like it there?' The guest was curious.

'Not much – it seemed boring. Too much amusement.'

'She finds everything boring.' The thin brother was part joking. 'And her job disgusts her.'

There was silence. Then she was replying.

'It should be good. On the radio. But you can say nothing.' The thin brother was taking her up.

'You should go out. Put on a short skirt, go to a club.'

'What – to meet people's husbands?'

It was an impasse. Sayd and Ali were grinning. Now the aunt was serious. She turned to the guest.

'Look, it's like this. Persian women can do nothing. Their fathers tell them what to do. Their brothers tell them. Their mothers side with their fathers. Men have sex in clubs and treat girls as play pets, interchange them, discard, or keep and betray. Well, it's not always like that, but often it is.' She was attractive as she spoke, animated, black hair hung across her face and her figure showed as she stretched in her chair, elegant. 'And of course we have to be religious, read the Koran regularly, pray as our fathers indicate.'

'Yet, the King is also a pleasure boy.' Sayd was smiling again. 'He has his rich palace, does what he wants in it. The business men from abroad, they too want pleasure, money. They're blind, babies, or else entirely cynical.'

'Yeah, and he uses Evin to keep it all safe.'

Again the silence fell. They'd all seen the prison in its suburb. Once you were in you were lost to the outside, you were nameless. You could be dead, or lying battered into a stroke or brain disease, no-one outside would be kept informed. Maybe in a year a relative would be notified. Or you'd be taken away, your relative would come to look at the prison walls, maybe daily, outside, but you'd not be in, you'd be a thousand miles away. Or you might be dead. Or a hostage in a basement, chained.

The others were clearing the meal. They'd sat on the floor, eaten off a rug. Suddenly he realised that Zohre kept these truths at bay and dreamed out – she was as aware of her social context as anyone he'd met. She just handled her awareness differently, keeping it away, remote. Maybe he was a route out for her. What can you do, you want to be happy, make an existence? Yet the context is at its deepest murderous, repression at a maximum. She might see what these people said as true, but think there was no point in saying it as no resultant came? What resultant lay in the future? He was back in the hot English lane. There was the nuclear research base. Everything was mixed, impure.

He wouldn't stay. They liked him to stay the night. He wanted to be back in his room; Zohre would come early next morning. Ali was easy in the car.

'Zohre, she is a nice girl. And her father will come round.'

He left the guest at the end of the alley, the moon lit up swirls of light snow, car tail lights swallowed up.

The Prince was back in the car, winging the streets. He'd look out from time to time, people looked low, dirty and foreign in the road, but he could approve the limousines that transported the business people, many from England, and the embassy was a useful point, kept up his luxuries.

And he'd done the shooting. A queer pride, he was a man, rose up. You killed someone, rightly, and you felt confirmed in your own manly self. It was like in the helicopters, you shot off rounds and saw the heaped mounds, dealt death British army-style. Then there'd been the fucks with the small girls. True, they were wogs, he'd have preferred English girls, but they were better than nothing.

'The Empress gets them. From her nursery schools. There's a supply.' The first King had told him, whispery with his lingering English.

'So fuck on, fuck on.' He was shouting, beating at the glass partition, to get the embassy driver to get round a blockage. It would be the airport, home.

And it was in the bag, tank deals, those little vans too for going in the street, mobile detention centres, little torture cars. They'd be good in England, he'd pack in the low, like hippies who listened to queer music and wouldn't get on, union men, maybe unemployed people too, he knew the type. Everyone he met got on, he was shouting at the driver, 'Get on, man, get on,' and he'd give him a slap when he got out, who gave a fuck, it was officer's rights. And he'd kneel to his mother, sweeten her up, the cunning old regal bitch fixing to go to a murderer's banquet here in Tehran. And saying it was part of a sales drive! But no-one knew, or minded as sales were respectable and a kind of obligation, governmentally encouraged at any cost and beyond all consideration. And the murders were necessary, to keep order, he had respect for them.

He was twisting in his room, the father's friend. His wife was moving, plump, in the kitchen, he heard her voice rise as she spoke to a relative, he'd rather be in a night club with a prostitute. The nuts glowed in a glass bowl set out and suddenly they were flying all about the room, he'd booted out. The women's faces peered in, then went away, he heard the talk resume, he had his moods.

His debts were mounting up. The girl's father would provide more capital. And there was the deal come up, he'd be in, it was on the edge of royal provision, a building at the prison. The father had put it his way. A queer feeling rose and he was heating up a lump of opium on a round metal plate. He'd do a favour, tell a father his daughter was in danger of becoming a whore to a foreigner or he might not put it like that, you didn't know, it might backfire and the father beat him out of the house and call his debts in. It was a dilemma. He could see the nuts scattered, some were lodged round the wheels of a gold trolley the television was on. He called his wife in.

'Clear them up – those nuts.'

'Clear them up yourself.'

'Your duty is to clear them up.'

'And yours is to go with prostitutes.'

He was drawing in, the opium glowed on its tray, you picked up the lump with tweezers and then inhaled the fume through a tube. He was skinny, his wife thought, like a man from the boneyard, back from the dead. Round the corner of the door the relative's face poked small and queer, through the fume she looked like a fox or fairy he couldn't decide.

Suddenly the opium tray was banged across the room like the cymbal of a drum kit flown loose and the small glowing drug cube was lodged down with the nuts. The television was showing the English Prince at the airport, Henley the Minister too, and there was talk of the Prince's mother, the English Queen, perhaps coming soon for the Persian Royal Festival.

The man was up, standing erect for his king, it was dignity at the airport, he himself served his own king. Then he was down, grappling for the drug. It seemed stuck, half burnt into the carpet. He was running double, very calm and beside that, parallel, very fast as thoughts spun. His wife looked at him, maybe someone would fondle her in the train sleeping car, like in Amirshahi's story she'd just read, while he slept; outside a moon hung over an adjoining villa, the rich zone.

The door slammed. He'd gone. She was used to it. He'd be at the clubs, she was at home with her relatives.

He was panting in the road. He'd calm down, ring the girl's father. He knew how he'd put it now. He'd say, he'd met her boyfriend and how nice he'd seemed. Her parents wouldn't know about it, ask him more details. That way, he'd done a favour, but not seemed hostile, kept his position, even improved it. The father would be angry. And his wife, he was softening, he'd make it up to her, not make her clear up the nuts and bits of broken glass. He'd go back, make the phone call, then make it clear he felt wrong about the nuts.

The wife could hear him at the phone in his room. There was anger at the end of the line; he himself, bony, spoke calmingly, 'perhaps there was no harm in it', 'had thought it best to let you know', 'you can now act for the best'. So, he was at it, breaking people's happiness, harming young people for his own gain, securing advantages for himself. She could glean it, it was a daughter, she'd chosen a man for herself, tried to make something happy, here, in this hell place. She'd seen the army out, that morning – her own brother was in prison – rushing people into the British vans.

Her husband was out of his room, calm and pleased. She was looking. Suddenly she was running, a hot opium block between her fingers, jabbing it in his eye hard, pressing it in. He jerked back, giving light screams.

'You hate love. You hate everything. You hate me. You hate yourself. You're a prison builder. You brought the British vans here.' She was accusing him.

It was true. Even in his pain he felt some pride. He had organised, for the King's army, the contract with the British for the military vans. He'd even gone to Coventry, vile place, to complete the vehicle deal. She was running again, the red glowing opium block was at his face but he caught her arm this time and bent it back to the point it might crack.

'You don't like the vans because they put your brother in one. He had no decency. They strapped him down inside and operated on him. The blood ran out of the drain grids I ordered to be installed, my own modified specification, over in Coventry. What of it?' He was twisting the arm so she was bent, face to the floor, near the nuts.

'Now you've got a prison contract. You're wrecking a girl's hopes. What are you, simply sick?'

Her mouth was near the nuts and he could feel his eye burn and bleed.

'Eat the nut.'

She was chewing, the carpet loomed close, a little burnt, where the opium had stuck. He was leading her about like an animal on a tether to where the nuts were, making her eat.

'Each nut is a truth. It was my religious duty to inform a father if his daughter is in danger of sinning and ruining the father's name. The next nut represents service to the King and loyalty, welcoming his friends here like the English royals and honouring the political and business guests, also from the USA, who accompany them.'

She was crawling, forced, from nut to nut; Islamic truths

THE PERSIAN WEDDING

as he saw them were contained in each one and some nuts had business truths in that needed emphasis. The last nut was the van her brother had been tortured in. She felt her mouth crammed with nut flesh that she couldn't swallow like when he'd crammed his penis into her mouth after smearing it across her face on the wedding night and choked her almost unconscious.

She was up, 'let's kiss' and she was spitting the nuts back into his mouth as he was biting her face into red slits, bringing his hand round for slapping her head.

The Englishman was dreaming. One self he brought with him and set down here. It had nothing to do with here. He was sick of the self, wanted to kill it off. She had come with another self that was used to being here. It was herself, as she was. The selves lay about, how he'd been educated, brought up, what feelings ran most frequently in him. That was one person. She also had her views, feelings. How did they match up, come together? Could you fit them close?

And all along the energy ran to fit him together, there were perceptions, reflections, things he liked and didn't like, feelings that made you anxious and disturbed or else pleased you. He was assuming, he'd done well, badly in other ways, split down the middle like a half cracked stone, maybe. And how was she, unified or not?

She was wondering in her room, while he dreamed. Sometimes he didn't seem to relax, he was caught up in – it didn't seem to be thinking exactly – registering, feeling things. So he walked in the road, taking it all in, the traffic that burst and polluted all around, the tawdry shops in bare concrete frames, the swathed men, poor and ominous. Why should he, why didn't he absorb himself in her, how her lips curved and hair hung? He should separate out, see things different. But he was as he was.

She didn't think consciously, aim like some girls for a pristine flat with white sofa covers, that was beyond their pale. She felt the sofa would distance her from him. But what she expected was herself too, part of her. She wanted to be happy with him. People dwindled down, became a sum of small material things. She didn't want to be like that. Then there'd be the sensual ecstasy, some kind of fluid that bound it all together, made one of all the separate modes and tasks. How was it, how could you put it all together?

But now she loved him as he was. If he registered it all, so be it, it made up for all those who saw nothing. She was sad too, maybe he wasn't happy. Something deep in him struck her as burning low, keeping him down, maybe low moods came too often. She was sympathetic.

The flat was warm as usual. It was the evening. The Englishman lay on the bed, in emotional suspense, and lit a cigarette. If only Zohre was here now! But she had to be at home. The evenings alone began to alarm him. She was apart, in her home. It was like a secret zone, he had no access there. It was coming to dominate, he wondered, like an excluded area that was unexplored, but crucial. She didn't talk about it. It was all queer, he was foreign, intruding, seen as this perhaps, if her parents knew of him. She'd come in the morning. He was always waiting for her.

The bell rang quite early, at nine. He went to open the gate. It wasn't Zohre, but Nasrin, her sister, He saw her, looking curiously through the gateway as he opened the outer door. He hadn't seen her since the summer in England. Since he arrived he had arranged to meet her again, through Zohre, but something had always happened to prevent the meeting.

He remembered her now, back in England, in the hot summer. She had an intelligent way of speaking, also she laughed and smiled very easily. He had come across her, sometimes, in the old library in the college. The sun slanted in through high windows, there were the gardens and fields beyond below. She was reading a book of Persian religious poetry alone. They both liked to sit in the spacious Georgian room, looking out into the sun across the lawns to the fields.

She was confused to be discovered there, afraid he might laugh at her, proud. He hadn't known at first that she was

Zohre's sister. They had talked for a while, she explained the poem to him. Zohre had told him her sister was religious and often prayed at home. It was a way to retreat from the family, to obscure her father but also to please him with the observancies. In England it had been strange, at first, to associate this girl with prayer, because of her warmth and laughter. Maybe they ran together, he suddenly thought.

Now he recognised her again, though she seemed changed. She looked thinner, less buoyant. She smiled at him, then looked worried.

'Zohre – she couldn't come. She will come at twelve. My parents say she must go to the university.' They walked on into his room. She kissed him on the cheek in greeting and he kissed her in return. They were both very pleased to see each other. He registered what she said, would hear later from Zohre what it was about, a shadow passed.

Nasrin turned to him, warmly, speaking quickly. From the start there had been a tacit understanding between them, a quick mutual liking and respect. Both felt they could really be friends.

'If you and my sister are married, I will be very pleased. I want this.' She trusted the man. 'Whatever you say, is true,' she added.

He smiled back at her in reply.

'Yes, I want to marry your sister', he told her. But he felt overpraised, speaking true was hard, didn't always happen, he supposed.

He liked this sister very much. She worked as an accountant, training, for the National Oil Company. Her mother worked there. She had wanted to study philosophy but her father had advised against it. She lived at home, too. Now she sat on the chair by the door, in his room, drinking tea. It was the first time she had been there but she showed no surprise.

'Zohre has told me about everything here', she explained. She looked round the room, then turned back to the man.

'We must go to the university soon, meet her there.' She changed the subject. 'I'd never been to this part of the city before this day.' She was excited to be there. It didn't matter that it was more basic than she was used to. He saw her again back in the English garden; now they were here, doing this. Things moved. He had kept his promise to come, wanted to. Now this was this.

Her words and gestures were lively, kind. Her vitality flowed out impulsively. She wasn't acting up to an image of herself. Then she looked worried again. 'I hope my father will agree. I pray for that. There is a good chance. And the prayers bring fate onto our side.'

'He will agree', the man replied, confident. 'And I'm glad to have the prayers.' They looked at each other and laughed. The high metal door slammed shut behind them, they were out in the street to wait for a taxi.

He was waking up, gradually, standing there in the street. He would like this girl to be his sister. He wanted the commitment of that relation. She would visit him and Zohre very often, make visits, even to England again. With Zohre he would move on, into a warmer, more open world. He was excited as he thought of this movement, like a release. His blood ran faster, the release was definite. Nasrin too would be part of it.

A taxi stopped, they got in. Nasrin looked out of the windows with interest, alert: this part of the city was new to her, she wanted to see it. She pointed out what interested her. Suddenly she turned to him.

'I will help you and Zohre all I can. That's for sure.' He knew she had already given Zohre money to help pay for the rent of the flat. She would help both of them. She was looking at him, more serious now, it wasn't money but something more, spiritual help and force. She would help both of them, it was definite.

The taxi stopped by the university. They stepped across a wide, shallow ditch running with quick flowing water, to reach the pavement. The snow was melting. He helped Nasrin to balance on the big stones that broke the water's surface. They went in through a doorway, upstairs, to a café. 'Zohre will come here at 12,' she told him, and disappeared down the stairs, back to her job, across the city.

Soon he heard Zohre come through the outside door, he recognised her steps. She looked very beautiful to him that morning, there in the café with her black hair shining, her skin glowing with warm energy. He loved her acutely, as he saw her. She brought with her an atmosphere and impulse that was essential to him. She smiled at him, with real care. She had been hurrying. She moved to his side and stood close to him, showing her connection with him to the other Persian students. As they went down the stairs she kissed him warmly, her eyes looked teasing.

In the street she turned to him. She was composed, but by her eyes he could tell she was worried. She almost trembled, beneath a tight control that kept her outwardly calm; he felt her subdued shaking. Sometimes she hid her pain from him and he didn't notice it. His recognition moved in fits and starts. He wanted her to tell him when she was upset, but a strong pride and habit of concealment made her try to hide it. But also she wanted it recognised without her saying. Now she spoke,

'Yesterday my father and mother came home from work, very angry. They wouldn't speak to me.'

All this time she had been keeping the news to herself. He looked at her, wishing she had told him earlier. She hadn't been able to tell him. Anyway, he had no phone and even if he had, she couldn't have used her parents' or gone out alone to a call box to phone him. 'So, I knew what was wrong, they knew about us. My father's friend had told them, that we'd been to his office and he'd seen you, us together.' She spoke with control, on the surface, but below this angry with her father's friend.

'He rang up almost as soon as we left, or not long after.'

She was agitated in the new confusion. 'So now my father must decide. He must talk about it with my mother and with me.' She seemed to accept the events as things she had no power over.

The taxi they were in ran on between the concrete apartments, the landscape was hostile and ugly. Nothing out there in the systems would help them. She swayed against him in the back of the car. He knew they should have kept away from her father's friend. They sat close, consoled by the contact.

'Your parents would have known sooner or later anyway.' His words were pointless – their closeness was the real answer.

Zohre sat very still in the car. He felt her softly flowing into and around him as she rested against him, a new energy. She was thinking, a long way off, about her family, her father. The foreign man didn't understand her absence, her strange quietness. Her hair brushed his face as she turned to him. She was already his wife. Everything had taken place like a gift. There was a force in the background; they had been given to each other by a power beyond themselves. There was the attraction as a root: what happened now was their responsibility only. The sun too had burned them together, the English dark where the twigs and brambles had poked out in the wood, they'd been sanctioned. So he felt it. They had to interpret the gift. She looked at him, quietly, with trust. He longed to move her closer to him. But also she was close. It was weird, how could her father and mother in any case have any say in it all, apart from being pleased such a contact had arisen. And anyway, what was wrong with himself, what could be objected to? There was nothing. All would go well.

The taxi was moving on. There was a new element now, to be in. Some kind of control was gone and others were working them, or trying to. It was odd, why should her parents be allotted powers of approval or not? Of course it was a custom. Fleeting fragments of things half built filled the car windows, a kind of grey sickness stretched. The city was murky, lost in remote meanings, torn into separate zones of belief, words blew like vacant flags, religion, the west, spies, prisons, collusions, breakages, the place spun just violent and divided. Meanwhile in rich flats and villas families ate meals, talked. People were divided, separate behind walls which missiles or bombs could smash in seconds. It was the final point of argument to blast away opposition to yourself. There was a man creeping and bearded, a zealot, another man in designer shoes and western suits, they passed, mirror clichés. A family was respectable, Islamic saints on the walls, a daughter should behave, there were precepts.

Zohre was clutching his hand, there were things to fear. As they got out of the taxi the snow had begun to swirl, where you are makes you vulnerable. How was it, did they have more options, back in the wood in the English summer? Maybe here the balance shifted, she had her room in her parents place, he had nothing. True, his job would begin, he valued that and so did she. But what kind of counter was it to the breaking meanings that swirled on the pavement where they walked now? Rich dictator, religious zealot, the free market – choose a lost meaning and fuck up whichever way you chose. Hatreds swelled up, whatever, there were tortures and vices to go with all of them.

Zohre was looking at him. He seemed lost. She wanted him back.

'Do I make you happy? I want to.' Just then he felt anything but happy.

'Yes, you do.' It struck him as cruel to explain the rest. He didn't do her justice – she wouldn't have cared that his mood was dark. A burger bar loomed up at the roadside where swathed men ate and a line of military vans were discreet up a side road. She held his arm tight and he put it round her, they would combat it all, go away again if they needed, they were strong.

'And I will make it all right with my parents.'

She was looking at him convinced, as she spoke.

They were back in the actual, crossing the five lanes of traffic, holding hands across the carriage way. A bearded man looked stern, across.

She'd have to go back, her parents had set a curfew. And next day was a Holy Day. If her parents went out, she'd come to him. They'd be discussing, her father might consult with relatives. For now she'd kiss him hard on the mouth and the bearded man could look on, biding time, running a fantasy through, that the streets would be his to purge of sin, and not that far off in time. The streets would run with blood, arrests, beatings. It was a dream and he could be thrown in jail now for voicing it, real enough, oppressed. Then his blood would run.

They went into a café. It had to be brief, she was due back. There wasn't much else to say. They looked at each other across the table. She drew him in. He hated it when she was upset. He wanted to go with her, at once, to her family. What was the point of the delays? His own parents would have welcomed her, without issue. What was the point of this other protocol? What purpose did it serve? He was stranded in a separate place. What would happen, what would her father say? He felt rich and confident of her, in any case.

He wanted to talk to her. Somehow it was hard, they didn't communicate like that. She would look at him, or touch his arm, they understood each other. But he wanted to say things, ask her about her family, what she felt.

Today they were driving. There was ice on the buildings, the taxi curved into a quieter suburb, the edge of the private university she studied at. The city drowned the English wood out, the hot summer was then, this was now. And all the time the present was being overtaken. Something was slipping, wasn't being envisaged.

He turned to her. She looked all that he could want. She was smiling.

'So, this is where I do my studies.'

She seemed not to care so much about them.

'What do your parents want you to do?' He was smiling back. She looked into the distance.

'I don't know. Sometimes I don't understand them, what they do or want.'

He looked at her, concerned. She always made him feel tender towards her. But he didn't know what to make of it.

'So I go in my room at home.'

'And what then?'

She looked at him, slowly, in the eyes, shifting the ground.

'You know you are the best thing that happened to me.'

'It's the same for me.'

'So – we will be married.'

She was pleased. But then she looked worried.

'And my father will agree.'

'Why shouldn't he?'

He was thinking. Why should they be obstructed? What she thought he couldn't get hold of, it was what he wanted to understand. What could she do, by herself? It seemed the father hung up ahead, a fact that influenced that he knew nothing about. Zohre struck him as unknown at these times, it bothered him, there was something he should know but didn't.

Once she came unexpected to his flat that she felt was theirs. It was a holiday, her parents had gone out, she was free to come without them knowing. She was there, in the icy yard, kissed him hard. She looked at him without saying anything, he looked back.

'So Ali and Sudabeh will take us to the mountains.'

The car swung out of the city, northern suburbs, picked up speed, cross country. Bare spaces of land stretched flat. Sudabeh was explaining, her parents too had gone out, she could come, Otherwise she would have had to stay in. There were complications, she spoke quietly to Ali, who knew about the older man she saw. The car filled with cigarette smoke.

Zohre leaned against him, A line of parked cars on a summit with snow each side of the road made them stop, park too. There was a restaurant, people sat outside, sunglasses on, faces to winter sun. She was adapting, she fitted where she was but there was a line of tension too that was constant, her family put it there.

She walked with him in the snow.

Again she was saying it.

'You are the best thing.' He looked back at her.

'And so are you – for me.'

Some kind of tears were appearing.

'You know – it is so horrible here. There is violence, people get beaten. And maybe my father is involved. I don't know. Someone makes him be. He comes to our house, a thin, rich man, the translator we call him. People talk, we can't do anything.'

'Maybe we should leave, when we get married.'

'We can do that.'

He was surprised, usually she was level, didn't admit when things ran negative. All around the high peaks crowded in, and she moved to hug him. He held her and they both saw the peaks that separated where they were from movement on. You could cross them into Russia and move oblique west, you'd get to Vienna, all the places, Zurich, a centre. It was always possible to move. But you were encumbered, always, where you were with systems and things to clog you up.

She was always hoping, so was he.

'It's more complicated, than in the summer.'

She laughed.

'We are used to that. Everything is complicated here.'

He could go into it, the influences, embassies, England. Sometime he would have to tell her everything he knew. But it never seemed the right time and maybe it was true, what was the point. These facts bored him.

They walked back. Ali and Sudabeh sat at the bar, talking. In the distance they looked animated.

'He would marry her.'

'So why don't they?'

'She thinks of the old man also.' Zohre was joking. 'Us women – we all want a comfortable life. That's why I'm with you.' She smiled.

A small red sun dwindled over the peaks, they moved down the road in the car now, dusk was coming. It had been a relief to be out, the city was ahead again, they'd be back in. Another way, Russia, Zurich – it would be adult to leave. She wanted to go with the man, start new. The other places would relax her, here all was jittery, too much was unexplained, out of awareness, covert knowledges hung all around, power and money set secret scenes, lines of harm ran in. He felt the pressure run in his body, latent, explosive, it might come from outside, sellers, fathers, blockades the systems put in place.

*

He was dropped off and walked up the alleyway back to his room in the dark, no-one around. The buildings on each side held ordinary lives but were unfamiliar in a way that disconcerted him. The rules seemed small. He didn't understand them. The city didn't encourage him. His job began in a month. For now he had hardly any money. He didn't count here. True, he had some friends. But he was reliant on Zohre, her movement to and from the flat, her mediation. Violences ran in the background, secret rules, religious practices, secret circles, things were abrupt, breaking off, rebegun, or not. You could vanish in the street, a body might be handed over later, also there were complete vanishings. The evenings alone in his room were trying.

Now he was also angry. What right had Zohre's parents to keep her at times in the house? Why did she submit to it? Why should his own life and hers be hampered by these restrictions? It was all one way, he had no power, conventions and her parents' views ran things.

He was wondering. He unlocked the gate and crossed the courtyard, uneasy. The night seemed edgy, presences ran that contradicted each other; thick polythene sheeting flapped in jerks around the switched off fountain in the yard. Why should Zohre tolerate the pressures of her parents? Why should her father be involved at all? Wasn't there some other, more objective spirit to serve? But where would she have learned that? Maybe all her life she had been brought up to submit to the religious father. Yet he wasn't religious, he did deals, grew rich, was commercial. Maybe this wasn't the whole truth about her family. Her parents could be generous, kind to her. But she was held back by them. If she challenged or disobeyed them, her parents could say 'Go out if you don't like us, go away.' And no Persian girl lived alone, without her family, here. She wasn't able to question them, without the threat of losing their affection, of being thrust from the home. In England it had been different, she could do as she liked. So what would happen? She was to be swept about from an impulse to be at one with her family or to be at one with him.

He sat down on the edge of the bed, It was time to sleep. He lay down, a kind of sad anger flickered. He wanted Zohre to understand him. He was afraid she wouldn't want his perceptions. Anyway, he might be wrong. And she wasn't blind; her eyes were open to something different. With her he moved into a different world. In the end she was mysterious; she had a subtle power that spread over him. He felt strange to himself when she was there, she woke him up in ways that surprised him all the time.

It was getting light outside. An old man began to wail in prayer up an alleyway. The younger men woke up. Zohre had said she might not come today. It was a holiday. If her parents went out, she could come. Things were hung up. It was a day to get through. The next day she would come, for sure.

Zohre rang the bell, He let her in through the gate. She was breathless because she had been hurrying. She bent forwards to kiss him on the mouth. She moved quickly towards him. She was happy, looking forward to something. She went into the room and sat down, looking at the books scattered around.

'One of the teachers at the college, she has invited us to eat with her and her husband. I told her we are getting married.' She smiled, excited as she spoke. He smiled back, looked at her. She seemed vulnerable in her happiness. She went on.

'My father too, he has been talking about us, to my mother, to friends, asking what they think.' Her face fell slightly. The happy mood wasn't total. She was too proud to tell him directly, was strained by it all.

'You know, yesterday, my parents were going out. So I got ready to come here. Then they didn't go, so I had to stay in. I wanted to come.' She looked at him questioningly, had he wanted her? She came towards him and he stroked her hair as she sat close to him.

'What can I tell my father, to help him to decide? '

It was hard to answer. He didn't know what the father needed.

'You must tell him what you want to do.'
She looked disappointed.
'That wouldn't be enough.'
Suddenly she laughed.
'It will all go well. And you have a job.' She was pleased that was fixed. 'You don't smoke or drink, you are educated. What else is wanted? You are a good Moslem.' She was teasing him.

He moved away from the bed to make tea. Zohre went to the table, took a long roll from her bag and cut it in two. As he crouched in front of the dented pan with the water in it on the hotplate, he saw her as she arranged the table. Her hands moved unconsciously, she was absorbed in the task, contained in her further hopeful world. She made him feel proud, they would be together. She laughed.

'You look like a savage, there, with the water.'

She came quickly and sat on the floor, her hand on his shoulder. She kissed him on the side of his face, teasing him.

'You can cook all my meals for me.'

It felt so remote, this flat, like a hiding place in the city. What they did had no reference to anyone else – how could it involve other people? They were both carried on by another, private force which could either be acknowledged or else evaded and betrayed by others.

They drank the tea in bed. It was lunchtime, when they felt ready to move again. They had both slept. He had dreamed, he was on a hillside, a fortune-teller directed him and an old woman in a black chador had waited under low fruit trees with a mountain behind. Everything was alien, it was Zohre's grandmother. Short grass was an unfamiliar green, it was miles from anywhere he knew. Then it was the English wood with a steep lane curving upwards between arching trees and just in front of him a thin fox crossed, its fur tough and worn in patches, emerging from a hedge down a bank on one side, disappearing. It was indifferent to him.

'Let's go to a café,' she said.

They got up, banged the high metal gate behind.

A taxi dropped them near the American Cultural Centre. They walked along the street, went down the stairs into the café he'd come to with her the day he arrived. It was a reminder, seemed months ago. She caught hold of his arm, He smiled at her, looking at her fresh, honest face, her eyes that showed her love for him. They sat at a table. The lights were green, turning everything green. It was quite dark. She sat opposite him. If they both leaned back in their seats they were too far apart to talk. She sat forward and so did he. The place made him uneasy, she balanced him out.

'So what shall I really tell my father?' She asked him the old question again.

'Does he have to be told anything?' He spoke quickly now, looking at her gently.

'Yes, then you must come to the house to hear what he says, after I tell him I want to be married.'

These were the marriage procedures, as she knew them.

'What if your father says no?' He asked suddenly, as if the thought had just occurred to him. It seemed impossible there could be an objection.

'If I tell him I want to marry you, he will give me reasons, for or against. And I will tell him I want to.' She spoke as if the events had been often rehearsed in her mind. The family procedure was so familiar to her she couldn't grasp easily it was alien to him.

'What if he gives you reasons for not marrying me?'

'Then – I have to think of them.'

She looked aside as she spoke. She was afraid he would be taken from her. Would she resist her father if she had to? She trusted her father to respect her emotions and choice, he would be on her side. Yet the foreign man was unhappy. He had no real control over these important things. He'd be put in the balance and judged. He didn't know the basis of the assessing. Why should the father be the arbiter?

'Why do we have to do like this? Your father, why has he the right to judge, then do as he likes?' He was indignant, it was humiliating, to allow her father to judge him, like a product or a business plan.

'You must come. Then he'll decide. He only wants what I want, what is best.' She repeated the steps in the process dreamily – they were part of her life, facts to obey. He mistrusted the dream.

'It seems stupid to do it like this.'

'Then everyone in Persia is stupid.'

'Perhaps they are in this case.'

They sat silently after this exchange. Something vital was running out of him, some source of life. Zohre sat, vaguely hurt, slightly sulky. So, he didn't love her then. He was unkind to say these things. Why should he object? She sat, brooding. She looked at him slowly, touched his hand on the table. She wanted him back in their usual world, spoke to him.

'I would do everything for you.' She always said this: it made him feel he wanted to care for her in some crucial way, be vital to her. No-one had ever spoken to him like this before.

She was looking. She knew sometimes he hated it out in the vicious streets, she could sense his recoil. She hated them herself, just was used to it all. And in any case she could use her father's car and driver. Her movements were circumscribed, within limits and order to and from the university. Yet she had been sent as well to the college in England where she could do as she chose. She was thinking.

'When we are married we could go – every weekend – somewhere else, north of Tehran, to the sea, to my father's other house. And then we could go to England.' She looked thoughtful. 'But you should not say to me, go back to Persia, to visit my parents and not come yourself.'

'I wouldn't say that.'

'No, but some men would. And European girls do as they like, go around alone.'

Somehow a confusion was setting in. They would discuss more. She wanted him to fit himself to her and he was trying. Only it was hard for him to accept her father as arbiter. She trusted her father to respect her feelings and wishes, she didn't doubt him. Yet, the other man knew, there must be anger in her father he wasn't showing except on the first evening when the father and mother had stonewalled the girl, acted silent and offended. Things had twisted together wrong. They could be corrected, put straight, it wasn't hard.

Now they would go back to his flat. Zohre could be there just briefly. It was already late, she was expected home. On the pavement she looked at him, upset. Her eyes were hurt, imploring him. The customs just had to be gone along with. Maybe things were breaking open for her too, she saw her father's power in it all differently now. It was a stress to deal with. She wanted to talk to him more but now she had to go. It made her feel sick. Things were shortened up, a kind of wave at home had been set in motion, it would flow out. Was it like fate, God's will? Her sister believed that, she didn't. Her father would consider her.

Were they the idiots then? He was suddenly asking when she had gone. They could sidestep this linear path. What was the need to advance directly to marriage, to undergo assessment? He could work, she could meet him. She just needed to speak to him, discuss, so they could make out other oblique moves. She too was perhaps also set in the precepts, this advance towards a climax, but she was flexible, they could change. What was it this moving on in phased advance towards a fixed goal? They didn't have to do it like this, could move to be married their own way. Protocols mixed with fixed ideas of a passage, progress on. He could get her to duck from these, they could take their own route to be married.

Or maybe not. He looked round the room. It was limited like the path set out ahead. No-one was going to step aside, budge. He'd have to go forward with the expected process. Maybe it was prefixed, he was bound to fail. He didn't know. It was like a gamble with execution. Some kind of snares were perhaps being set. He didn't know if he held any good cards, the pack might be marked.

Vaguely he wondered why they were putting themselves both through it all. Common wisdom, religion, set out the path. She hadn't thought it would get risky like this, hadn't envisaged what was released, potential judgements, dismissals. Violence was all around. Within it as a context you had emotions, followed paths, you were squeezed. There were other violences, father, daughter, family rules. Maybe violence was human, making pressures, credos, restriction wherever. Or somewhere things opened out, there was just calm and warmth, love.. He doubted it. The norms in England were no better. It was as if they were all cursed and in this place the curse took on a novel maximum. Doubtless where he came from had its own bad maxima. There was no way out, just to go outside it all. He wondered if she saw the need as he did, outsiders were easiest of all to pick off.

He thought too of the marriage table: how many miles to Evin? The torture screams would be invisible but hang in the air, sound shapes, unheard. You had to be happy come what may, live your life regardless, it was the London mantra as it was here, dance in your room as the outside exploded.

This was good. Behind the thick green curtains the snow swirled, falling fresh. He was going through with it all, withstanding, a queer forbearance here in the foreign zone. He'd do it for her. But he was being pulled on into a dangerous area, the risks were high. She should be more aware, listen to the warning notes that were all over. Maybe she felt secure in her home. It was a refuge that was real, necessary. He'd not been there – it would be the assessment zone, the climactic place all their paths lead to. No-one would alter procedures, step aside. He would give himself up to the process and he wanted to be married to her, they would go forward now. He knew she didn't much care about the tenets either, they were just a means she used to reach the end she wanted, to marry him.

His mood waxed and waned, he was confused, was unsure what views were valid, things swirled about.

He hated to let her go, back down the alleyway to get another taxi home. She walked away, round a corner. All he could do now was wait for the morning, to clear everything up, her to come back.

Things had been taken out of his hands. What he and she wanted, apparently, was subject to another power. He had no way of knowing what Zohre's parents would say to her. She would be back at home now, listening. He wished he had given her more courage. But she had enough of her own. He wanted to go at once to be with her, resist what they said if they were against him.

He couldn't conceive her home, pressures that could be put on her there. It was mysterious – the family was in possession of a code of thought and behaviour he was excluded from. He felt that he didn't count, to the parents. To the father he was a factor in a situation; there could be no actual consideration of what he was. The father had never met him. But the father could be fair, he didn't know.

The oil stove hummed at the side of the room. The lamp lit up the long green curtains pleasantly. He couldn't feel at ease. Something was about to happen, some outcome. He went to bed. He knew Zohre would be there in the morning – they could talk again, plan things out, how to do them.

When he woke up it was late. His head felt heavy. He got up and sat down at the table. His movements, he realised, were becoming ritualised; the room was so small there was little possibility to vary them, in any case, There was nothing to do. He wanted Zohre to come, badly. He hoped she felt the same and would arrive early. He imagined opening the door to her and seeing her standing there. She would kiss him as she came in.

He went out onto the veranda to collect the butter and milk he kept there in the cold, for his breakfast. The courtyard was covered in water and the polythene wrapping over the fountain was coated with bubbles of rain sliding across the surface. The place seemed bleak, temporary. He felt unhappy. Things moved slow. She must surely come soon. He sat down at the table waiting. Soon it would all be resolved.

Midday came and passed. No-one had come. He felt his spirits bleeding away. The room offered nothing – there was nothing outside. His circumstances were perverse. It was only because he wanted her to come so badly that she couldn't come. There must be some problem at home. He connected the problem only vaguely with himself. Perhaps her parents didn't want her to come out to visit him until they had seen and approved him. Then it would be all right. But there seemed something strange in the air, a bad wind blew, coming from a secret centre, a zone he'd not been in. She lived in the north of the city, the King's palaces were there, a black spirit was flying, there to here. Out in the yard the drone of a plane made him look up, red lights flashed on the wide wings, it was bringing people in, England fuelled the dark, business, advice, weaponry.

He wrote a note saying he'd gone to the shops and stepped out into the rain. He stuck the note on the outside of the door. Some children sheltering in a doorway watched him curiously as he stood there jamming the note into a crack in the metal. When I'm back she will be here, he thought. He walked in a blur of sensations to the shop. The streets were the same. Without Zohre he felt isolated in them. There was no reason to be there, without her. Persian script on the road signs and car registration plates baffled him. He felt estranged, stranded.

Walking back up the alleyway he saw the note still in the gate. It was wet now. Plainly on-one had come, He walked past the gate and carried on up the alleyway. The rain falling was a relief. He turned left into a wider alley that led onto the street. There was no-one about. He would telephone her university. She must be there. When he got to the yellow booth he saw it was occupied by an army officer. The man stood inside wearing a thick khaki coloured overcoat and a heavy peaked cap. His boots were heavy and black with a metal reinforced toe section. You could kick the suspect til his stomach broke open. A tiny union jack trademark projected from a seam above the heel. He was talking animatedly. Behind the Englishman other people paused to queue.

His hold on events was slackening. He was exposed and alone now. Zohre had helped him to do everything. Now she had vanished. He stepped into the call box. She wasn't at the university. He would try her home. She was there.

'Nasrin will come for you tonight.' Her voice sounded strained and tense.

'Are you all right?'

'Yes, I'm all right. But I can't talk now.' She was replying, blankly. He knew something was wrong. He couldn't imagine her home, the secret zone she spoke from. Maybe her mother stood next to her as she spoke.

She repeated, 'Nasrin will come tonight.'

'But what's happening?' He wanted her to tell him. A young girl in a black robe tapped impatiently at the glass. He ignored her.

'Tonight, wait in your room. Nasrin will come. Goodbye.' She sounded tearful.

He left the booth, confused. What did it mean? Perhaps this was part of the Persian custom before marriage. But something must be wrong. He looked forward to Zohre explaining it all, later. He trusted her to do that.

Back in his room the afternoon passed slowly. He lay on the bed, smoking cigarettes, waiting. Suddenly he realised the order of his existence, with Zohre, was being broken up, leaving him stranded. He thought of the last discussion they'd had, in the café, bitterly. It had been a waste of time, done harm. Maybe it had reduced her strength. The terms were all wrong, now he was being summoned with no choice to a situation he didn't understand. It was even combative, the father worked it all. Already his daughter was depressed. The father's friend begun the sequence. Now absolutes were all about, explanations at a zero. A queer system of beliefs circulated, oppressive. They'd been jammed up; now they poured out all around, dust released from obsolete rooms, poisons from broken open containers. He was even a target. He wondered how much of this Zohre knew.

It began to get dark. The bell rang. Nasrin stood at the gate. Her eyes were serious as he swung the door. He didn't understand her look. She kissed him on the cheek warmly.

'My father – you must come tonight to eat with us. The driver will take us.'

They went across the wet courtyard into the room.

'I have been praying all afternoon. What my father decides, it is for the best. But I want you to marry my sister. It would please me.' She seemed strained, as if she had been part of an emotional scene, particular and intense.

'It must be fate, what happens, what God wills. I believe that.'

He looked at her curiously for a moment. He didn't like this identification of the father's decision with God's. Faith was risky, misleading.

She went on. 'I don't know what my father has decided. Whatever it is – it is for the best', she repeated.

As she spoke, she didn't look as though she believed what she said. She looked helpless, without power. He believed that she had been praying for him and her sister. He felt a warmth of sympathy and liking for her. In Europe it would be a joke that she had prayed, whereas he liked it. She had tried to help him as hard as she knew how. He valued it very much, that she took it all seriously.

She looked him over.

'You must change', she said, smiling at him. She looked quickly round the room. 'Put on this.' She had moved towards the clothes stand and was pointing urgently to his suit. He reacted against her urgency. It was her father who was the cause of the new turn of events. But her father had no power over him.

'Isn't that too formal?' She looked at him not understanding, a little puzzled. He had been trying to joke, find some stable point in what was happening.

He put on the suit in the bathroom, felt ridiculous. The absurdity distracted him. He felt strange as he got ready. He was going – where? What was the visit for? Was he to ask now if he could marry Zohre? Was it a visit to let the father assess his character? Now he was to go inside the zone he had been barred from, a secret place would be revealed. It had been in the background all along, a presence, right from his arrival, the phone call to there Zohre had to be covert about. For Zohre the place was real all the time, she went back there when she left him in the room. He was outside, now he'd cross the rim and be in there. The place was dominant. It was the destination implicit from the start. Now he was vulnerable, stripped of foreknowledge.

He was excited. He didn't know; what would happen now was out of his control. He felt too that now he was going to marry Zohre; he was preparing himself to be married, for the ceremony itself. It seemed unreal and desirable. He had worked hard, so had she, to reach this point. It wasn't an easy thing, to come here – and she had worked to smooth a path too. Now was the time for their efforts to take fruition, to make a climax. The emotions hurt and rocked. You didn't leave off, do these things for nothing. You carried forward. Maybe it all shouldn't involve efforts, ideal love drifted on. But in real mode, you moved through blockages, barriers were in yourself, his and hers, you burst or gnawed through. Outside obstacles weren't needed, they happened though, this was maybe one. Or a father might respect their efforts. The thoughts ran fast, speed mode.

He emerged into the bedroom, Nasrin looked at him.

'Your hair – it is always like that.' She moved her hand over her own hair in imitation. 'Put it like this – so.' She picked up her comb and arranged his hair. 'My father – he doesn't like men who drink and smoke. But you don't anyway. Not much. You must agree with all he says.' Nasrin's face so sombre, made him wary, defensive. He realised he didn't understand what was happening. A kind of passivity was coming on.

They walked up the alleyway. A large black American car was waiting. The driver opened the door. He was young, dressed rather casually, subdued, hid in his role of subordinate. Nasrin climbed into the back, familiar with the car, being driven. The Englishman disliked it, criminal's world.

It was dark now. The big car moved off slowly down the street, almost silently. It was incongruous, like a vehicle that had lost its cavalcade, where it would drive between outriders crammed with marksmen. Some sick violence hung about it. The engine noise was subdued, a discreet mechanical whine. Discretion was good for destruction. He sat back in the seat. It was a hearse vehicle, smooth like at his grandmother's funeral, high among terraced houses in a council estate above a west country port where nuclear submarines docked. This car's luxury was gloomy, like a quiet sickness. The big bonnet spread out in front, a black, wedge-shaped block of blank steel. It needed a flag, to mark out the dignitary inside, here come on a death dealing mission, weapons, covert operations, kings, presidents, high officials, royal trade envoys. Why was so much that belonged to wealth deathly? The car disgusted him, he jerked slightly, could there be blood on the seats?

Nasrin sat next to him, looking out of the window, thinking. In the car the rich man could glide along, untroubled by immediate contact with the ugliness he created and perpetuated to provide his wealth. Nasrin looked too good for the car. In her eyes and on her face was a glow of honest concern. She wanted him to be happy with her sister. She took his hand, looked full into his eyes.

'You know, I want you and my sister to be happy; I want my father to decide you can be married.'

She was repeating, added, 'And you should get out of all this. You hate the city, I can see that. It's full of violence, and hidden things. I hate it. But my family are here.' The Englishman smiled at her.

'It's true. But Zohre likes it.'

Nasrin was looking. 'She doesn't know she hates it.'

She changed the subject, 'You are honest.' She paused, 'And my parents have been asking – is he a gentleman?' She laughed, a little grimly. Things were surreal. Who was he to be judged against? The Royal Envoy for business, perhaps, the business officials for the weapons procurement deals, army advisers, corporate leaders, maybe a James Bond figure, all shits, and urbane, fighting confidence? What queer phantom idea should he be considered in terms of? It was shadow fighting all the time.

He knew his thoughts weren't useful, maybe he was exaggerating, he warned himself – the energy and motivation lay elsewhere. He remembered how Zohre delighted him. Above all he knew what it was like to be with her, the movement into the further life. His body shook slightly with pleasure, suddenly beneath his control. So he was going, and would marry her. It was decided. He was pleased with the decision. What he was doing felt very strange to him. He was in a car, travelling to receive a father's permission to marry his daughter. No tradition had prepared him for this. In England such customs were obsolete. Also he disliked business, wealth. Now he was going into contact with it, perhaps. Even that was unclear, the father could simply have borrowed capital for building projects and live among massive, constant debts. The father had several roles, covert contracts too for the government, the oil company. Zohre had told the Englishman one of her father's first questions about him had been 'Does he think we are very rich?' He could be seen as a seeker after money.

The car was running quietly along some back streets, deserted in the darkness. He turned to Nasrin.

'At the college, in England, when I first met you, you were reading some poetry alone in the library – do you remember? And then you spoke to me, a prayer from the Koran.'

He wanted to connect what was happening with its origins in the past. The summer wood seemed far back, an opposite. She looked at him, a little startled. For her the reading and the praying were normal activities. She smiled at the memory. But there seemed some deep fear in her, making her serious, the prayers would be tested now.

He began to feel strange, as if it wasn't himself in the car. He looked out of the window. The buildings were distant in the dark, outlines glimpsed roughly through the black glass. There were villas, low luxury apartment blocks set in gardens. Behind, miles off, came the snow peak glimmer of northern mountains. A few street lights blew dimly on wires at intervals. No-one was about.

He heard Nasrin tell the driver to go round to the main entrance of a block of apartments. Now they were close to where the family lived. He would be inside the centre of it all. Nasrin sat silent in the back of the car. She looked pained, resigned – she had no control over events. Her eyes were unhappy. She was caught between two awarenesses. She must obey her father, whatever he decided. Yet she knew it would be right for her sister to marry this man. She knew too what her father could do in the family to have his own way. He would be, the father felt, sanctioned in the Koran. He could not be contradicted.

She felt that the Englishman couldn't understand that it was impossible to go against a father's wishes.

'It will be all right,' she said suddenly. 'What happens – God has willed it.' She believed this. 'But if my father refuses – you must go away at once, back to England. It is better. Otherwise he will hire someone to follow you. Perhaps he would kill you.' She spoke tensely, her father was frightening to her. Yet she said nothing to him of her personal fear. He could use measures, silences, confinements, trackings, suddenly show up to check she was where she should be. But she could not speak disrespectfully of her father. She loved him too, he could be kind.

The Englishman sat still as the big car turned off the main street into a side road. They must be nearly there now. This must be the street. He was excited – he was about to enter a place which had been forbidden him until now. His letters from England had come here. The bare address took concrete form from the road and buildings. She had written hers to him in there.

The car was stopping. The street was no different from the other residential streets he had visited. It was quiet, spacious. A grey road ran straight between blocks of apartments. That was all. There was no time to gather firm impressions. He felt himself getting out of the car, following Nasrin to the door of a building that stood on the left, near the end of the street. The car moved away silently as they got out.

It didn't seem as if it was himself performing these actions, walking this short distance along the pavement. He was nervous, reluctant to go inside. The sister pressed the bell. Quickly he noticed the brass house number on the wall, the secure door at the top of a short flight of steps. The building was unobtrusively protected. It flashed into his mind that it would be hard to get into this building again if no-one wanted him in there. Nasrin spoke her name into the microphone by the door. The door buzzed and was open. They were inside at last.

Nasrin went in front of him, up a small flight of steps. At the top was a woman waiting to meet him. This must be Zohre's mother. She stood like a hostess, or warder he didn't know which. He noticed she looked beautiful in an older way. But the beauty was also social, in part, a jewelled necklace, hair coiffed, King's wife style. It wasn't possible to tell what mood lay behind the presented appearance.

She was subdued, as she shook hands, almost surly behind the brief smile. But also she was curious, who was he, who had come this far for one of her daughters? Perhaps it was real love. He felt dazed, he no longer knew what was happening. She led him into a room that opened off the hall. He caught sight of a low table, covered with flowers, bowls of fruit. Along a wall stood a dark, heavy sideboard. Things were arranged as if for a ceremony. Some nondescript pictures of religious scenes hung prominently on the wall, in ornamental frames. He didn't understand their themes, wasn't familiar. The furnishing seemed heavy, oppressive. Maybe it was his mood, he didn't see straight.

He walked in, wondering what would happen. Vaguely he was conscious Nasrin had disappeared. Zohre wasn't there. The mother was gone. He noticed with a slight shock that the father was sitting on a stool just inside the entrance to the room. He had his back to the wall. He would be out of sight at first. Now he looked heavy and obstinate. But he got up and shook hands neutrally.

*

THE PERSIAN WEDDING

The guest noticed another man sitting on a low couch. He had his back to the guest. He got up, turned and advanced smoothly to shake hands. He was tall and thin, late middle age, urbane and sinister. His hair was greying, he looked gaunt, somehow worn, like a dressed skeleton.

'I am – a friend of the family. This is Mr Ghani, Zohre's father. I will translate for him. They call me the translator.'

The guest sat on the couch, next to the man in the dark suit. Possibly this neutrality, so evident in the welcome, would give way to warmth later. He wondered where Zohre was, why she hadn't come in. The man in the suit sat posed at the end of the couch. He looked a little like pictures of the King, seemed to encourage the slight resemblance.

'I am also working for the national oil company. I translate there too. Where Zohre's mother also works.' He turned, smiling, to the foreign man. Something amoral hung in the air. His interests were vested in Mr Ghani's yet it also seemed the translator might have some control or edge over him. Fairness or impartial judgement felt remote.

A question came. 'How do you like Tehran?'

The translator was smiling, urbane. He'd asked this a thousand times before, sellers and business guests at the company, meals to fix dealings. The mild smiling manner was useful as a mask at business meetings – here it grated on the foreign man.

And, in fact, he had asked about the man, back at the oil company. A seller had come, high profile, an outrider of the Prince envoy's group. They'd got chatting. Henley had stood in his English suit and he'd stood too, the translator, in a black suit himself, while the King's group had sat aside, making the negotiation documents.

'A young Englishman, here, to marry my best friend's daughter.'

Henley was grinning, his face stretched in consideration, weighing up.

'What do you think?'

'Has he money?'

'I don't think so.'
'Has he studied?'
'Yes, but humanities only.'

Henley was going to ask where. He couldn't be bothered. And if at a high status institute that would only complicate things. He'd avoid the issue.

'If someone comes here with no money it can only be a bad sign. Anyone from a good family or worthwhile would have money, naturally.' The latest statement was a central tenet Henley held, also politically.

The translator agreed, it was what he privately thought. Henley was going on.

'And if you ask me, the world would be better off without such people. Certainly not to let them in to upper circles which they could only misunderstand.'

Then Henley was grinning. Thin lips drew back round his gums, little teeth ran neat round the bone. 'I know what I'd do.'

'What?'

'Send him packing as a little shit.'

The Iranian was shocked, to be so explicit was risky. But he felt the same, better so. Only let in the upper circles to privilege, those who can understand them from the right point of view. He stole a glance, sideways, Henley was heating up, it seemed some point of torsion had been reached from which some crisis might emerge, an explosion of views, 'science is great', 'get me my dumb boy to fuck', but the seller was controlling back, the torsion was settling, no capsize was going to happen. Henley was grasping the Persian's arm, warm, taking his leave.

'And your deal will rid you of shits here.'

It was the weapons, the Persian nodded, well bought, the English killing fields. 'It's science, maths, products of truth.' Henley was insistent on these points.

Urbanity was devious, like a lie, the younger man was thinking. The living room loomed round, an unfamiliar context. Who were these people? They seemed to believe their money and business activities entitled them to respect, deference and the right to control. One was a father, he would control his daughters, make them follow the right way. The guest was replying.

'It's an interesting city. Of course it is crowded.'

The banal reply was appropriate. The translator spoke in Persian to Mr Ghani, who fell into a heavy silence.

The atmosphere was suspended. The wife came forward with tea, pouring it into small cups. Zohre came into the room at the same time. She came in inconspicuously, as if not wanting to be noticed. He saw her with a shock. Now she looked strained and faded, trying to obliterate her presence, ashamed, in the room. She looked only downwards, not at him. She looked up unhappily once or twice, her glance was mingled still with pride. But she was gone, far off, he sensed it. She was dressed very differently to usual. She wore old corduroy trousers, her appearance was unusually disordered. She wore no make up. Usually she dressed finely, took much trouble. Perhaps she had been called a whore by her parents. The guest didn't know. Now she presented herself badly, hurt herself. She didn't speak.

He looked at her briefly. It was a painful look. Her eyes usually shining and vivid, were now dull, turned in. He felt he was hardly there for her. Clearly something was wrong. What was happening? If this meeting was to give the father the opportunity of judging him, why was there the mode of veiled hostility, suspicion? It was hard to follow on and he was deeply sad on Zohre's behalf.

The oil company man was talking again in Persian to Mr. Ghani. Another question was coming. It seemed rehearsed, what would be asked.

'You're interested in culture – in literature and art.' The translator turned, smiling offensively. 'Here you must find much to interest you. Persia is so cultured.' His tone implied that he was familiar with literature and culture and such inwardness was an element of his manner. 'The Shah too values such things and appreciates them.'

'Yes, I enjoy literature.' The guest felt the answer would be received as a weak point. The hearers had no use for it but must appear to have appropriated it as part of urbane show and rote remark. He was deliberately vague.

Suddenly the guest realised the questions had all been planned beforehand and were meant to make him appear undesirable, get rid of him. How could he handle this? Zohre sat crushed, listening. She would not dare to join in. The dark pieces of furniture stood neutrally about the room. As he sat the colours intensified, deepened, blackening like bad signs, moved into his body. He was getting heavier. The place was alien. He wondered if Zohre knew what her father and his friend were doing. She sat unhappily on a chair near her father's, her face frozen. Her father never looked or spoke to her. Her expression was stony and fixed. He felt unhappy – what had brought her to this? What had her parents done to her, what words were said?

He realised with a start that the elegant business man was probing again.

'I expect it was awkward for you to come away from your own country, and leave your classes.' The question really meant, have you a job at all. He hadn't got one back in England. What did it matter, anyway, the outer world of work? These men would serve it on and on, be judged respectable. He had to calculate an answer, appear to endorse their reality. 'I have a teaching post arranged if I go back.'

The translator passed the information on. The father looked up, his look was surprised. So, the young man is not a parasite. The stolid, stubborn man was also Zohre's father. The guest must make an effort to please for her sake. He spoke, looking at the father.

'I mean to work here too. I've been offered a job at the university. It begins in a month, when the work permit is through.' The oil translator looked alarmed. Who knew if he relayed the information right back to the father? And in any case such a job was nothing.

'Ah yes. It is hard to get permits. You see' – he lowered his voice in respect. 'The Shah, rightly is afraid of those who are against him and civilisation. They come here, otherwise, from abroad and make trouble.' He sat elegant on the couch. He would serve any system, for his own advantage. If the Shah went, he would adjust his allegiances fast. He spoke quickly to the father, who nodded in agreement. Both men looked at the guest, he might say something, compromise himself, make their plan go easier. The guest was agreeing, 'Yes, certainly, the social forms mustn't be undermined.'

Zohre sat annulled. The Persian men took no notice of her. Her discomfort was a matter of complete indifference to them. Whatever she had felt for this guest was irrelevant, it had no bearing on anything here. They wouldn't understand what had happened in England. In any case the West was there to be used by them as the West used them. At root they disliked and resented it, what it assumed. The guest could understand that. The miserable, withdrawn girl, the man they were trying to catch out – they were irrelevancies. The main thing was to keep a limited vision intact, seal themselves in. England was similar. Small, mean men with limited, selfish imaginations created the norms. Men like these were who society rewarded. It all fed round, circular. And you could do down youth into the bargain, make genuine attraction into an indecent thing, destroy it as it showed. The sterile framework replaced it, hung in everyone's face. In England you would allow the attraction but the frame was the same. And people were hung up there, sex was a focus, something to gloat over, exploit. It was all fear, the basis.

He sat on in the ugly room with its heavy furnishing and objects of status and was powerless. Something was being done, spiritual rape, a kind of psychic theft. The men's power was real. And they were taking advantage of him, his position as a foreigner, a guest, his inevitable ignorance. He was vulnerable, in Evin prison you made someone vulnerable, stripped them down, then you did things to them, you took them over. The West provided equipment and advice. A world of sick meanings floated in figures round his head.

There was the girl's stony face and subdued manner as a product of their desire to protect themselves at all costs. What had she done wrong? What rights did they have to make her ashamed and submit to their view. Yet she loved her father too. He could be kind. It was hard to attend to the process knowing her conflicts, answer the questions. He couldn't help her here. If he could talk to her she would love him. These men knew that too. They were determined she should not. He didn't believe completely they could be so cynical, so decidedly against him. They knew nothing about him. Perhaps he could still win them over.

The mother came in to sit down. He was conscious she was looking at him with the appraising eye of a woman. She sat next to her daughter, yet she would go along with her husband's views. She valued her material status, was no free spirit. Zohre had told him at first her mother seemed pleased when she knew about them both. But then she had grown less enthusiastic in the discussions that followed. The mother smiled briefly at him with some regret. She was meaningless, an elegant object, she might have been well-disposed to him but now sided with her husband. It was good behaviour.

The translator finished his conversation in Persian with the father. They were easing off, cruelty had its own flow.

'I expect you will want to take back some souvenirs to England with you. There are some gold trays, golden things, silver ornaments, carpets in the bazaar. Other business visitors take such things home.' The translator thought of Mr Henley, loading his luggage with thick gold bars and jewellery. Was he wealthy or not, came the probe. The two men waited, suspended for the reply.

'I haven't been to the bazaar. When I'm there I will look out for them.'

In fact he had no money at all. In Tehran you needed it. He had a promised job. But in any case he was expected to go away, leave the land, maybe with a gold bar in his luggage and no harm done, nothing raped. Can you be raped in your head? He was wondering. He felt sick and low now, taken advantage of by the men and used like a victim dragged into a thicket and forced to have sex. They were violating him hard. He saw Zohre was powerless yet he wondered why she should be. No-one would overturn these tables unless it was the father. The guest supposed the older man could smash up his own room to show displeasure if he chose, make his women feel dirty and soiled. Once he had run into Zohre's room, torn the bedclothes off her bed, ripped her clothes from hangers and flung them on the floor. She had been ten, had never forgotten his rage. Some queer attitude lurked in which the spirit was damaged, smirched over with omissions, misinterpretation. What were they so afraid of?

It was time to eat. A guest is to be honoured. The Islamic creed says so. The table was arranged in the other half of the room. He walked over to the place indicated, uncertain. Waves of unreality came over, who was he, here? The translator sat down next to him with the air of a guest who is familiar with the organisation of a particular household. A kind of weariness hung about him as of a necessary duty, a wisdom to be applied.

It was dark outside; the room was lit gently by several lamps. Zohre sat on the other side of the table, not opposite him. She said nothing, kept her face turned down. She looked very young, sitting there. She looked sulky, angrily resigned. But all was subdued, switched down, a key-note tone. She didn't look at him.

The guest realised that all his attention was meant to be given to the father and the family friend. There was no way to relate to Zohre here. She was cut off from him by the presence of her parents even though she was only a short distance away. She cut herself off, duty as a daughter. Her emotions must be switching about as she sat. He sat uncomfortably at the table, powerless and insulted. Still he would sit though whatever they had to say.

The translator drew some dishes towards the guest.

'Look at all this food that has been prepared for you by Mrs Ghani.'

Some comment of appreciation was called for. It struck him as strange they should expect and seek for compliments while engaged in cheating and misleading him themselves. In any case they were set on exploiting his ignorance of custom, convincing him their behaviour was the norm. The meal started, flatly. He had no appetite. Zohre was eating nothing. She moved her fork wearily round her plate. He was caught up in some separate place, apart from her. She seemed to have chosen to be defenceless. How had her parents changed her to this? What did she think of their persuasions? She would tell him everything tomorrow, that was sure. The belief sustained him.

He didn't doubt, as he sat, that she would explain, that she would find a way to come to him to speak. That kept him on, sitting there, replying. He could see she was having difficulty swallowing the food. He knew her. Sometimes, she had told him, I cannot eat at home. He was remembering what she said. 'My father, he took me to doctors. It went on for six months.'

Suddenly she was putting her napkin to her mouth. 'I'm sorry – I feel sick.' She moved fast from the room. A kind of silence fell, the furniture seemed to lie more heavily about the place. The mother looked across at the father, sudden. Then her eyes were back on her plate, looking down. The father stared ahead, powerful. The translator was making a joke.

'Ah, young women, young women! Eh, Mrs Ghani. My daughter was just the same.'

A brief silence came.

Zohre was coming back. Silently she moved to the table, resumed her seat. She looked pale and exhausted. Her mother gave her a quick glance.

The translator was speeding up now. He adopted a mild tone, querying but easy, tentative.

'Why didn't you ask Zohre's parents about their daughter when they were on holiday for a week in London last summer? You could have gone to see them then.'

Zohre lifted her eyes quickly and spoke for the first time.

'He was working. How could he have come?' She fell back into silence. It seemed odd to the guest that it was just over that point that she made some protest. He didn't understand. It was the only time she spoke.

'Yet he was not far from London.' It was the first time the translator had spoken to her. Something was hidden here.

The translator was smiling now, offensively polite. Now they had caught out the Englishman and the daughter. The translator waited, alert, business-meeting style, for the answer. The Englishman had been relating to the daughter, deceiving her parents, even while they were in England, under their noses.

The father didn't like to be deceived. He recalled how Zohre had seemed unusually happy visiting them in London. Her mother had asked her often, 'Why are you so happy' and had no reply. He was angry with the foreigner. And suspicion of sex swirled round, it was bad morality that had happened, there could be family shame; marriage was for the body. Something that was disgusting perhaps had happened. He backed off, couldn't go further, a sort of doubt was creeping in, was it really disgusting, points of faith were being threatened, was he being unfair to the younger man?

The guest was replying simply. The questions were absurd and unfair.

'Yes, I was working all the time.'

'You could have saved money, the plane fare, if you'd met them then.' The conversation tailed off, a hiatus.

'Mrs Ghani is an expert accountant. She can type very fast.' Suddenly the translator produced this information, which hung incongruous over the table. He was switching subjects. A statement of appreciation was again called for. Conversation was moved on, calculation, deceit and the gain of an objective were all.

They moved back to the settee in the distant half of the room. Zohre and her mother cleared the table, went to the kitchen, did not return. The meal was over. Now it was time for more direct talk. The translator begun. Cultures were incompatible, he claimed.

'There are many barriers between East and West.' Now they would pretend to proceed by reasoned argument, to justify themselves. The visitor knew any objection they raised he could counter and destroy by arguments of his own, reference to legitimate, energetic emotion, even logic. But nothing he might say made any difference. Different criteria were in play, he should be kept powerless.

'The family is different here, much closer. In England you put all the old people into hostels, no-one cares about them.'

The guest thought of his own parents, now dead. He had cared for them both. Was a close family one where a daughter threw up her food at mealtimes or choked when she swallowed?

'Besides, you are of different religion.' The translator was going on, enumerating. 'Mr Ghani is a very religious man. You see those pictures on the walls.' He pointed to reproductions in gold frames. 'They are all religious images, saintly scenes, martyrs of Islam. This family is very religious. So you see it is not easy. You would not understand the pictures. There is all the family to think of, the grandparents in particular.'

An unintelligence swirled in the room, fogged it up. Was he to be insulted in these ways too, expected to swallow the arguments, unchallenged? It was strange to realise they did expect this, for him to accept the points, to respect the father as a religious man, to acknowledge these factors they cited as final, clinching. The translator had passed on the contract provision for the military torture vans from England to the father's friend who had then grassed Zohre up. A guest was being tricked. It was against the Koran. Islam was for honesty and friendship in its highest form.

The translator went on.

'It is a disgrace for the daughter to marry a Christian. The other girls would in consequence be unlucky.'

Zohre had told him before her parents might want him to change his religion. She herself couldn't care less. Even so her upbringing had been in Islamic terms, she was influenced.

Her sister prayed, the guest knew, it was valuable, a fine thing to respect. He respected it. Zohre had spoken of her parents' views jokingly – you must be Moslem she told him – she didn't imagine they'd take a stand, stubborn, against the younger man.

Was she surprised by her parents now? He looked at her briefly – she was dazed, obliterated, silent. Perhaps it was a contradiction – could she modify her sense of her parents now, because of their behaviour here? Or would she have to love them at all costs, regardless of what they did to him or her?

He didn't care about changing his religion. What did the outside forms matter?

'I could change', he told the translator quickly.

'It takes time, some years.' The translator was lying. In fact, the change could take place very quickly. The prophet would accept you fast. Back then, out in the desert, in the past, the allegiance was often made right and swift, you could decide in a fast shift of revelation. The prophet would not like this lying in his name. The guest held the liars in a cup and looked at them small, showed them so the prophet might smile in contempt at them. Who was who, religious, not religious, change it round! Some kind of peace came brief as he had the thoughts. Even, he thought Mohammed was with him in support. Whatever the guest said, however accommodating he was, the cruelty would go on, the lies too, hard.

The father was muttering in Persian. He turned and spoke to Zohre, sitting next to him, subdued and exhausted. She was very pale now.

'You must decide', the father spoke.

She replied out loud in flat English. 'I cannot decide. It is for you to choose.' Maybe she was trying to tell the Englishman she was not responsible, she couldn't help what was happening. He felt exhausted, also blanked out.

In her hand he noticed she held two rings. She was nervously fumbling with them. He felt a rush of love for her, anger at those people who made her suffer. What had she done wrong? Her monotonous tone sounded defeated. Maybe her father would have a qualm of conscience now. He went on, the older man, in Persian to the translator. Nothing definite was yet said, but it appeared to the guest the evening was closing.

The translator began again.

'We will travel back in the same car.' The mother stood at the door, holding the guest's coat. He put it on, still disbelieving what was happening. Zohre was there. She stood with her eyes downcast. She held out her hand and looked at him, openly for the first time with an appealing look, not to be hard on her. She was sulky, resigned. She looked ill and pale, she spun in it all. The mother shook hands. He was leaving. He found himself going down the stairs, his body was shaken, apart, and the door closed behind him.

Outside it was cold, snow fell, light, the black car waited at the kerb. The translator got in, sat beside the foreign man. The car started. Now they were away from the house the Persian man could be explicit, abrupt. The urbane manner diminished, an unsmiling, razor face loomed, thin at the top of a bent body, long and looping.

'Could you tell what the father's answer was? You could see he wasn't pleased. Do not be angry.'

He placed his hand on the younger man's arm.

The refusal seemed absurd, to be reversed for justice to be done.

'You cannot marry Zohre.' The translator was explicit again.

'And what does Zohre think?'

'She thinks as her parents.' The reply was glib, thoughtless, 'Man proposes, God disposes.' There was no problem for the older man, sum it up in a cliché, a rehearsed task now done.

The car was stopping.

'Good night, I get out here.' A thin arm was extended to be shaken. There came a pause.

'Mr Ghani can help you book your ticket back to England. You can give him your passport too.' He spoke with menace, subtle, some threat was in the offing, implicit. 'I advise you to take his help. The car will collect the items tomorrow. Give them to the driver.'

The man was gone. The Englishman knew they'd only feel safe when he left the country. They'd supervise him out.

All this time he had no doubt the next day Zohre would come and explain everything to him and they would plan what to do next. It was the thought that she would come the next day that sustained him, bore him up She would be there.

The car ran on through the dark streets. The driver drove faster now he was alone with the younger man. The Englishman sat in the back, angry and confused. Of course Zohre would realise this was unfair. She loved him. She would fight for what she wanted. His anger subsided as he realised that tomorrow he would see her. They would plan what to do.

Why should he be bothered now? It was pointless. The streets were dark and wet. The car stopped in the road next to his flat. What was he to do now? He could only wait. He got out, walked down the alleyway. Now unlocking the gate was a miserable act. The flat seemed obsolete. It had begun as an area of hope. Now what was it? Still, tomorrow she would come. Some kind of theft and violation had happened, he'd been attacked, she would make it good. A low physical mode began, he was sweeping down, something was shifting, breakage.

He went to bed wearily, not knowing how to arrange his thoughts. He was blank, disbelieving. He was overwhelmed by the injustice. How could the father be so calculating and composed? Feelings were taking him over, he could feel a long, low downward pull begin, grey water rising heavy, drawing in strange currents. It was like being overwhelmed and borne off. He must marry Zohre. He slept fitfully.

Then, suddenly, he was awake. The room was pitch dark.

A kind of distant noise, rattling, alerted him. There was a locked door that lead to the rest of the house his room was part of. Vaguely he was out of bed, saw the knob twitch. He pushed a bolt across. There was scuffling, a sinister voice, intoning in Persian. Perhaps it was a dream; through the curtain slit he thought he saw two men in black robes stand just inside his gate; or was it robes? It looked like some kind of combat gear, jeans and military jackets, guns slung below. Maybe it was a warning or else the room would next swing and slide with flying dark shapes that swooped or rise and burn in a bomb blast. Perhaps the prophets had come to view him and decide how to act. There might be new verses to recite. But he was unimportant, he supposed, they wouldn't come for him. The room rocked with a kind of queer extra darkness that hung from the ceiling and came to clothe him, put a kind of weight down. Were the men real? He looked outside, the courtyard was just visible. There was no-one now. Things were sick, he was weighted down, whatever had come moved now in fast descent, a sorrow to capture him.

He woke up, impatient, too alert. It was ten already. The thick curtains had stopped the light from waking him. Some kind of fume was in the room as if the stove chimney was partly blocked. Maybe the men had done it. But anyway, the thing was old. You could lie dead in the room then be shipped out, loaded in a crate in a big jet's cargo hold. He was lethargic now. He would wait for Zohre. He knew she would come. Time passed. No-one came. His spirits sank lower. Maybe she couldn't come out. Vaguely he knew she would be under surveillance, maybe tailed. Everything was gone under, submerged.

He put on his coat and walked in the rain to the phone box. He dialled her number. The mother answered coldly, passed him to Zohre. It was the same flat tone.

'Hello, how are you?' She was speaking.

'What's happening?' he asked quickly. Her flatness disturbed him, made him all the more anxious and insistent.

'Everything finishes.' He stood in the booth, listening to what she said. The mammoth city stretched around, he was one tiny point. He spoke urgently.

'Can't you come here to talk?'

'I cannot leave the house. But it doesn't matter. It must finish.' She spoke the words with a dead, flat insistence, repeating them to herself. It was as if the plan her father had initiated had taken root in her – now she too had decided her response in advance. Her words were like instructions she repeated but believed in. Her brain was shutting down with the stress, thought was collapsed and shot through, emotions twisted up and down.

The man felt powerless in the booth. The city swelled alien all around. What could he say, to counteract this?

'Well, that's unfair. I came here for you.' He stopped, realising the reply was stupid, like a child's complaint. He was desperate because of her flatness, emotions swung like a grey sea in a swell, memories burned vivid in the massive heavy water, floating fires. Even so, the unfairness disturbed him, the injustice of these events. What reality did they fit?

'I cannot talk now,' Zohre told him urgently. Someone was telling her to stop. 'Ring me tonight, at six.' He heard the receiver cut the contact.

The street was superfluous. He looked blankly at the people waiting outside the phone booth. There were always queues. The people had no connection with him. Without Zohre there was no point in him being there. He had no function in the city. She had come to meet him in the flat every day, had met him at the airport, they were in sure contact. Now it was all taken away. But could this outcome be final? She was essential to him. He knew she should marry him. The evenings in England meant she should be his wife, they were burned together. Nothing could deny that. But also it was a fact. The denial had been made. The contradiction was brutal.

He got through the day in an unpleasant daze of thought. Perhaps at six she will have changed her mind. At six he made his way to the booth. This booth was now his only link with her. Only their voices could be exchanged. There could be no warmth, no contact, just sounds. What she said was monitored. He would have to make the call in full view of the waiting people. He heard her speak down the wire.

'You see, I suddenly felt I didn't love you. At first I told my father, yes, I would marry you. Then I changed my mind, as he talked to me. He was angry at the beginning. So I don't love you.' She was trying not to cry as she spoke. She went on. 'I thought, today, I wanted to go to England with you. But now I think I love my parents.' She was crying as she told him. He knew she still loved him. Why had she listened to her father?

'You only say this because of your parents.'

'No, I decide for myself.'

She wouldn't admit to any influence. There came no criticism of her father. Yet her parents had made her set her love for him against her love for her family, her place in it. Her sisters would suffer if she married a foreign man, the family would lose status, there would be talk. He wanted to be with her, to explain, convince. She continued.

'You must go back to England. This morning' – her voice faltered – 'you didn't seem to understand anything. I don't want a divorce later. I must marry a Persian boy. Someone who is of our religion.' She was crying, 'I have tried to make myself busy, all day, to forget ...'

Outside the booth people waiting grew impatient. A woman in a chador rapped on the glass with a coin. Her yellow teeth pressed at him from the black. What could he say back down the line? How could he find words to counteract the influence of her parents? He had five minutes in a phone booth. Her parents had days to work on her. He didn't want to force her. All day she had to listen to her parents' persuasion. He knew she would feel lost, between her family and himself. He always felt kind to her, she aroused it; she would be suffering. He was too. And someplace he blamed her for not resisting. It was all stupid. Why couldn't everyone back down, compromise? He could go for a drink with her father, have a good evening, talk things through, make jokes, they could come to see each other clearly. And in it all would be the serious, empathising purpose.

Why was he the older man's enemy? Would the prophet have really wanted this conflict, mistrusts stirred, fixity instead of some empathy of view and feeling? Why should there be conflict now? They all walked the earth, men, there was the same end up ahead. What was the point? If the prophet himself swirled now about the phone box, materialised urging change on the back car seat next to the father, it would make no difference. The old views hung on while the prophet had moved ahead. His interpreters were locked down, dealing with the obsolete, while he danced in advance begging for new insights from his interpreters. Maybe the past tenets became themselves sin and the devil, they hung you back. Who knew, if you saw ahead, if there had to be prophets, Christ and Mohammed might link arms in a new, unanticipated radiance; what did God want? Maybe there were also other unimagined ways. There might be quite other prophets and revelations ahead, nothing was final. How could mere men know, anyhow? The speed thoughts came .

He was talking, too.

'We wouldn't get divorced. Why do you say this?'

There were no words to use, to send down the wires. She was silent. Then she spoke.

'You might tell me to visit my parents, alone, not come with me to Persia.'

'You know I wouldn't do that.'

'No, you wouldn't.' She was quiet. She had no answer for him. She was confused, afraid. So many words had been spoken now.

'Phone me tomorrow, please. I must go now.' She sounded sad and broken, crying again.

He found himself out on the pavement. It was raining and cold. The evening stretched ahead, meaningless. You found things out, how they went, then what did you do with the knowledge? Why had she done this to herself? What had her parents said to her? He was among very unknown forces and facts. He worried at them, insistent. He didn't want to become obsessed with them but he was getting so. His delays maybe had upset her, undermined her confidence, the discussion in the café too. He had spoken believing she loved him and the arguing wouldn't matter. It was discussing anyway, over points. Was it all his fault? Had he done something wrong, along the line? Something vital was being wasted while he stood by helpless.

If she had really decided for herself, not to marry him what did that mean? Could her love for him change so rapidly? It was impossible. He remembered what they had done together. She had written to him every day while he was still in England. It was impossible to change like this. Why did she pretend she had? What was forcing her? As she spoke to him in the booth she had lost contact with what she herself was, obliterated it so she was unimportant. You made a cruel biography for someone else and cut your own autobiography into meanings that broke you up, gave you something to regret, put misery into your own world and other people's. Better to back down, reduce the pressures. Maybe people liked it, though, blowing up, explosions, watching wreckage fly and bodies lie cut and bloody? The Americans and English liked to sell and use bombs, loved these things, it was their element.

He was thrown back on himself. His response was his own affair, not her family's concern. He recalled her words, 'You must go back to England.' Was it so easy, then, to change, to go back? How could she think he could alter, 'forget' as she put it? She was in a dream, disembodied. In such a state there was no-one to relate to. He recalled how small she had seemed in her parents' home, shrunk, energy and vividness shut down. Yet when he wasn't there, perhaps she would be happy in the home. There might be evenings of the Persian dances; she would perform with her eyes highly made up and wearing the exotic, sensuous costumes. But it would be fake. The past days were over, it was war in the streets and between people, the English-made torture vans were running more and more, you couldn't take refuge. He was bewildered. Did she understand what she was doing and asking?

The flat was intolerable now. Redundant, it threw out at him the reasons why he had come there – without Zohre or the possibility of her presence it had no function.

He walked up the street. As usual it was full of traffic, the air fell heavy and polluted. Car lights cut though the dark. He felt very tired. A vital support was missing, maybe temporarily, he didn't know. He'd done all he could.

He would ring Ali. There was a vegetable shop up the street. He went inside, asked to use the phone. The man was helpful, friendly. Ali answered. He would come soon. The foreigner left the shop and walked back to the flat. Things were sped up, the events accumulated, but slowed down too so a weight spread throughout his body. He was exhausted, the thoughts were wearing out, leaving just the sea-grey swell of low feelings. The landscape reinforced his helplessness. Usually in the street it was jittery, a kind of anxious mode ran, the soldiers might appear for arrests and beatings, or some random explosion might happen. These events were getting more frequent. For now, he couldn't react, moved on just leaden and loaded out. He was anyone, walking in the street. The whole city was a financial construct; it had no purpose beyond being an area where money was made, political authority enforced. It was becoming a terror zone where people had parties and danced in old costumes or expensive western clothes behind frail walls that could be blown away. People were mostly in the same pattern, responses and evaluations determined in advance.

*

Where was Zohre now? She was at home, confined there. She was passed into his blood permanently. Her face was present in the people he passed. Girls smiled at him – how far could they take a man on, at what point did they stop, hang back, decide no further? When did their families step in? It was thoughts, they didn't move. Surely Zohre couldn't persist in the course she said she had chosen freely. Something had been violated. You had to remember right.

There was the footbridge over the rails at the small station in England. They had planned what they would do. It had all been harmless, some positive happiness to be there together. What reality had that been? Now it was to be shattered by frames of sin and the incompatible, religious reference? His body swelled in pain – what had he provided for her? His blood moved fully towards the woman but now the outlet was blocked.

The street stretched out. His grief was his own; meanwhile he must act as the rest, walk in the street normally, act as if nothing was happening. So, he walked in the street. Only three days ago he had been in that shop, with her – there stood the sacks of rice open, they'd chosen some, gone back to cook it. Then he had no inkling of this outcome. Had she? The question bent into his mind. She should have told him her fears and problems. She had been too proud to tell him. Her beauty seethed in his flesh. But he could not go to her now.

The flat was dismal. He swung the door open, blankly. Now the misery was low and settled, spread firmly over him as a constant. The room had been arranged by Zohre, not long ago. It was what remained of their plans. He sat on the bed, waited for Ali.

It was a while before the bell rang. It was dark. Ali understood the problem as the foreign man explained it. He listened warmly, while the Englishman talked, in the dark room. He was reassuring, in there.

'After a week she will come, leave the house. Now' – he shrugged his shoulders, 'she obeys her father, later it will be all right.'

But this didn't fit with what had happened. The events cut deeper. The crying on the phone, the fear, didn't suggest Zohre saw this as an outcome. Her parents were in control now.

'Come out to eat.' Ali was concerned, saw the other man as a brother. The men were similar. There was no point in staying there thinking. Both men knew the thoughts would come, in any case. The Persian wanted to distract his friend.

The two men drove off. Snow was spiralling again in the headlights. The Englishman thought of Zohre, kept in the home. There could be no relief for her. She must dread her parents' return from work, the renewed sense of her own guilt. Meanwhile in the day, someone kept watch, hired in. Her sister had vanished. She hadn't been present for the meal, nor to say goodbye to him. He hadn't heard from her. Now he acted from an upper self, pretending: the grief and anger moved into another form below, changing him.

One night Ali came again to collect him. Things were flat, depressed, there was nothing to say. The car bumped down the track leading to Ali's house, there was the flare of the gas burn-off from the oil field, miles off across the plain.

Inside Ali's aunt was cooking. She was indignant, the whole situation with Zohre sickened her. She had come back early from the radio station to do household chores. Now she wanted to speak to the guest. She came out from the kitchen, her eyes were alive, protesting. Now she was gentle, she sat down on a long settee.

'Did she not know her father? She should have managed him better.'

'Maybe she thought she knew him – he surprised her.'

The aunt was thinking. She smiled across.

'And for the fathers. It is sin they come up with, family

honour, some breach. The girls do something, the men drag it out from the Koran it is wrong. The girls get convinced themselves, even. They think they are bad, must repent.'

A kind of silence fell. The guest was tired, his head was struggling through it all, his emotions weighed him down.

'So what can you do when the girls get convinced?'

She was looking away.

'It is very hard. They want to please their parents. They don't want to seem bad to themselves, in their own eyes.'

He didn't say anything. She went on.

'In fact it is tragic. They ruin themselves. Their father wins.'

Sayd was calling out.

'The father mostly wins, it is true. And he backs it up with tradition, religious truths.'

'So, there you have it. We are often wretched. The girls pretend not, but it is so. They won't speak against their parents. Their emotions are divided up.' The aunt was sad as she spoke.

The room glowed in a low light, a stove burned in a corner. Ali had returned, in pajamas. He always changed after work. He was listening, quiet.

'And Sudabeh, how is she?' The guest was asking, sympathetic.

'She is split. Her parents want one thing, she wants another. Only with her it's different too. She doesn't know for herself what she wants. Does she want a rich man from the ministry or just me?'

'Maybe you'll be rich.' The guest was thinking.

'Maybe, I'm an architect. But it isn't the point. The girls are too broken up.'

The aunt was smiling, sad.

'I have no-one to supervise me. My parents are dead. I have no brothers. So here I am.'

The guest was fading out, the tiredness came in waves, they ate quietly, on the floor. The food was set out on a cloth. He'd sleep there, in a side room. The thoughts came. He saw the gas burning flame, glimpsed it through a window, he was far off from where he'd come from. It was like he'd been raped but there was no physical wound to tend and heal and recover from. So he functioned, apparently intact. The thing would go on, it would be unresolved, stay keeping everything low.

Zohre sat in her room. Her parents weren't speaking, she was in disgrace. She looked blankly at objects arranged on her dressing table, cosmetic pots. 'I must do as my parents want.' She repeated the words. She thought with the surface of her mind, not deep in. Her body was drifting elsewhere, dreamily apart. 'He can go ... back to England.' She was thinking. 'Why, it is better he goes. It is fate that this happens. God has decided.'

She saw briefly, there was a landscape of pain opening. She put the vision aside. Who was she, then sitting in her room? She was of no account. She was not herself. Her parents would look after her. Her life would be as before. She watched a shape representing herself move on into the distance. She would stay here. A door slammed somewhere in the house. It conveyed anger and her disgrace, she was shut out.

She felt weak, as if she was ill. Her parents had been persuading. 'We love you ... you must do what pleases us, for you love us. Think of your family and God.' She was biting the inside of her mouth til the blood came. Wounds moved you closer to God. She remembered England, the wood in the sun, the night before she left. He had been always gentle with her, he was as she packed, talking gently to her. Yet here in this city he had been unhappy, maybe. She was unhappy too.

She looked out of the window. A few orange lamps lit the street, in the distance smoke was drifting over the city centre, some kind of military gas to disperse people. A kind of searchlight was curving round. Because she was no-one, the man would be gone. She would take the punishment on herself. He had upset her parents, set them against her. It was too much to understand. Gradually she realised her mother was calling her in a sweet tone. Did her parents still love her? She got up, to go downstairs.

He walked towards the phone. The airport lounge was almost deserted in the early evening. Ali and his brothers sat lazily on one of the settees in the middle of the hall. Soon his plane would leave. Already the Aeroflot flight number was lit up electrically on the departure screen. It was flat, mundane to be here.

Her father's car had collected him, brought him to the airport. He had agreed to this final supervision. The outer forms didn't seem to matter now. The driver had come, there was no personal contact with any of Zohre's family. Maybe the driver had a weapon, who knew. The foreigner felt defeated, for a moment, by the father. Maybe Zohre still loved him, her parent.

Now the younger man no longer knew clearly what was happening, his emotions were blurred, disturbed by too much confusion. He was ground down. There was no question of the love departing. It seemed lodged forever in his blood. The love was him, now. A disillusion was fixing in him, because of these circumstances, below the surface, becoming part of his volition. Now his determination would be fierce. The love was real; it should be admitted, built on. Everything was reversed.

Zohre answered the phone.

'Where are you?' It was the same question she had asked when he arrived. He realised this, flat, another reversal.

'At the airport. Your father's car came for me.' He paused, 'I can only go now, if you promise you love me.' The words were wrong, incongruous. He should stay. He was reduced to coercion. Since the visit to her house he hadn't seen her. There had only been phone calls from public phone booths, from Ali's office, once or twice a day. She had wanted these. But she had never changed her declared position.

She was crying again.

'Yes, I love you.'

'I understand Persian customs now.' Why did he say that? He hardly knew what he said. Words were crushed out, he'd thought too much, emptied out meaning, run interpretation flat and down. The words meant nothing. The feelings were too confused to talk about them like this.

He was conscious of the Perspex hood, fixed to the wall of the lounge, over his head, above the telephone. Neither of them could explain what they felt. This was the father's intention, ruthlessly to break their contact. The younger man knew, it wasn't the end but the start of a process. She saw it as a termination, she was forcing herself to see it that way.

She was crying, finally.

'You must go ...' She put down the receiver. He imagined her beside him, to go back to England together. Was that reality wiped out?

He walked back to the group of men in the lounge. These brothers had helped him, taken him into their home, been solidly kind. There was an atmosphere of male warmth, friendship. No one said much. The boarding sign flashed on the departures panel. His plane would be out there on the tarmac beyond the doors, ready. He had to go.

Ali grasped both his arms. Sayd was looking sad. He came forward, mischievous. There were still bruises on his face.

'Remember this is Iran.' He smiled satirically. 'Our fathers are like the King ... But we can be rid of them all. Let us hope the clergy don't act like fathers too. For it's maybe their turn with power next.' The Englishman was walking to the departure gate. He was beyond the fence that divided travellers from those who stayed behind. Now he was on his own again. He turned, waved, went on, not thinking.

The city glimmered far off, over the barbed wire fence of the airport perimeter. Tanks stood in a field, ready. He saw the gun barrels with sacks across. Equipment from England, bought in. The city's triumphant ugliness – was it a final defeat? He would return. How could he reach her? Would she want him to come, see the need for him?

His departure was inevitable now. He was sealed into the plane. The evenings in England, their truth, must be stronger than these constraints, this place. A spreading disease was accepted as ordinary life. The truths, sensitive growing life, needed to be armed. Also Zohre would perhaps try to cut herself off from him. How to resist?

What was he returning to? There was the general, normal death in the west, complement to here. A white star tilted out of the window. Below were the orange lights. She was in his blood.

The plane climbed at a shallow angle. It was dark. Outside he saw the white moon, through the cabin window. The white, impersonal light lit up the cabin strangely, like a fierce sign. The plane was levelling now. Somewhere below, among the millions of houses, there she was. She would know he had gone, now. The new process had begun. He would come back later to try again. He must defend the new spirit. Nothing was over

PART TWO

Some distance off there were the ramparts, closing her in. She was lying in her room with the heat beating at the glass, early morning. Outside pine trees burned out their southern scent. French voices came. She wasn't from here, was from a long way off, it didn't matter. Some low gloom ran, that didn't fit with her outer self. She was only a woman, nothing would count. She was for fertility only. Perhaps it was so. Only she had her own thoughts; that must mean something. She wondered if they were stupid – no-one seemed to pay them much regard, Men didn't like women, except to touch them and make jokes: you were cursed to be attractive. She could swathe herself up, be invisible, if she chose.

Outside the sound of French voices rose distantly as the heat beat more into the room. There was a scrape of crates being unloaded, close to the kitchen of the residences. It was August, few students were there. She'd been here since July, would return to Tehran in September, learning French now. The days stretched out white and dusty, not quite empty, she had a few friends, but they were negligible, fleeting merely.

Nevertheless, she'd asked him to come, someone she'd known before, a few years back. He'd come, then to Iran. But her father had sent him away, forbidden her to see him. She was recalling it. It was shut down, cold, in her imagination. She hadn't contacted him since then, had let him go, hadn't even told him she'd been near in Switzerland, him in England, then. He'd thought she was far away. A queer passivity had gripped her, someone else was in control. She'd sat in classes, above lake Geneva, like a dream she lost herself in. It had even been pleasant to let everything slide, be away in the heat and overclear sunlight, the lake and boats, boring and below.

It was another country now, where she came from, different, torn up, no-one knew how much, it was over there. She was torn up, the experiences were too much, it all took place when she was abroad, religious men shouting in the road, mad acts. The Imam led, high in black, in a hard pulpit. Somehow it froze you up, you were alive, you had skin but no-one touched it. The Imam's canopy loomed like an obsolete funeral ornament.

She could see now her brown arms, their smooth skin with the white nightdress above, her black hair falling. She was beautiful, perhaps, she knew, people had said so but why should she care? The beauty was theirs, they saw it, not hers as she didn't feel it or belong to it. There it hung, extraneous, across herself that felt different. You could have children, babies; be fertile but for what? The religious men were marching, firing off their dirty matt guns. Surely a gun should be beautiful, not just a matt black rod, meaningless, mechanical? And she had sent the man away, followed her father's rule. Now she would call him back.

She hardly knew the man, though back then she felt she loved him. He had come for her, to her country. But she'd frozen it all up, since. She'd been younger and so had he – what had he done since? Outside the pines were hanging immobile and the sun was banking up, she saw it hang white, haze the sky up. She was blurred over to herself, didn't know who she was. But she moved as an element, could dress herself fine, be full of grace, take pleasure in that. It was all pleasurable, apart from in her mind, where the breaks in her society, in her past relationship, put pain she froze off. She'd caused pain too, he'd written to her, she'd not replied, not told him where she was. She'd been frozen up, but the affect had done harm not good, her femaleness had gone wrong and done it. Now, after three years, she was putting it right. She'd drift through the days in the inland southern sun until he came.

The King had poured out. There'd be a credit line from him, billions for England in its financial trouble. Who was he? A queer faltering was on him. He'd set it all up, poured money out before now on the English and American products. Only a few years back, they'd all come, heads of state, to the Persepolis party. There'd been the English Duke and a Prince, a future king, a Princess, secular leaders, the vice-president of the USA.

His mind was back. A trade envoy had flown in to show one of the newest British planes, a supersonic airliner. He'd ordered two, only a year ago. But it was running against him, he was to be a pariah now, he'd set up wrong things. It was puzzling, the USA and the English had encouraged him to be harsh and sold him the means to be it, trained him. But now he was to be left to hang. Some bearded man waited in Paris, he said he just wanted to return and be left in peace for his scholarly, religious pursuits. The French president had been at the King's Persepolis party. Now there seemed French movement against him. The French felt the bearded man should be flown back in triumph. Air France would provide a free plane. It would be a liberation according to the French.

It was queer, you shrivelled up at a kind of political power whim. And all was set up, the new person could take over this system of oppressions and even improve it, just run it on a different aegis. It was like a company take over, a new brand had its own associate ideas. Now it would be brand Islam. There'd be new directors and a new logo and mission statement. His would be partly reversed, the West would be out of favour.

'But who am I now?' It was queer, how did it come to be the opinion of the world leaders he was to be let drop? Already England and the USA were cosying up to the Iraq dictator instead, across the border. They'd back him now against the bearded brand, should that take hold.

It was odd, he'd had billions at his disposal and so would the new leader. He remembered his ride on the Concorde jet with the young millionaire English envoy and political aspirant. He'd spoken like a sycophant, curled hair and risen up, that Englishman, oily and insincere. How they'd grovelled when he'd ordered two planes for himself, the Persian King! And now the planes would never be delivered even though he'd paid. Maybe he had no thoughts and a kind of sickly film was spreading across his being and imagination instead, he was dying twice over, once from a growth that was being controlled and now from abandonment, replacement. Yes, they stood back, the English and the Americans, if that was their interest. And they came in, for you, if it was theirs too. He'd always felt more aligned to the English mode, at one with their royals. He had an Empire as they did, he had pomp and palaces, excess fortunes. The English Queen had entertained him. But latterly they'd drifted off, the Royals, seeing which way the wind had begun to blow, he was getting to be a pariah. The same would happen to his Iraqi counterpart, they'd build him up then drop him. It was the English and American way, betrayers, both.

What would happen to his prisoners? He supposed the new regime could keep most of them in the same prisons. And put in a whole load more, of their enemies. So it went on. You could pack in millions, those who were against you, chain them up in safe secret houses, keep them in basements out in the countryside, go in with clubs and beat their heads til no head remained visible, just churned flesh and bone. Or there'd be kickings. He'd gone himself, a mainstream prison, a man was held down, you stamped with the British boots on, steel capped, and the blood got hosed away by lackeys. There'd be Islamic events, punishment fests, just as he'd had purges and initiatives. It was dreary, his life had been a conception of royal ease and control, now control would have a different ethos. The kickings were for God and the people,

THE PERSIAN WEDDING

rather than for Western values. Somewhere things equalised, all became corrupt, rotted down to guards with minimal intelligence torturing a prisoner in a place screams had no listener. Just one captive, underground, a bunker under a field, a religious torture, a US torture, English, what was the difference, one or another, who gives a shit.

The mirror of the state room reflected him back; gold braids seemed to glitter in refracted sun across his hair, just a person, dying soon.

He was climbing, the Englishman, the road twisted round the hill, curving up. All around were trees, sparse in the late winter. A low sun gleamed, orange circle. Up above was the done up place. Now he'd been back a year. He was thinking of the Iranian girl as he climbed. He'd been ill when he got back. There were fevers, a kind of exhaustion. For a while he'd expected to see a letter from her on the doormat, he would crane round from his upper room, ill, to look below. But there was nothing, no explanation. Before she'd written often. Before what, he wondered, before he went. At least he'd been over there, got out of the enclosure and repeats of his own country. It was a long path back to health.

Now the road curved more. At the top had been the asylum and the carers had taken this route. The grounds would have been deserted, no-one allowed out. A mad English King had been locked up here for the treatments. Taken berserk in the spa baths he'd been rushed over in a closed carriage, round the crescents and across fields. It was strange, why should an asylum be on the top of a hill?

It was for the Arabs now. A kind of private recuperative area and college, the mad atmosphere was reconstructed out. It was part of a deal, aircraft equipment sold, private college training for the technicians. A Saudi Arabian prince had insisted on the hospital wing too. The Englishman could see white teeth, sometimes flashing behind a bush and someone grovelling for Islam on a muddy slope, head down to Mecca. He liked the prayers, they were something outside banality. It wasn't Persians he worked with here but Arabs.

THE PERSIAN WEDDING

The place was queerly demarcated, you came from Jeddah and learned airport technology, English for that, but in a separate wing were people come for the treatments. An Arab might pay very high for his boy, witless, to be shut away here, structured care it was. He'd seen the boy in wrappings strapped to a central pillar in a room while his mouth grimaced and body shook.

Yet his own instruction area was set out, luxurious. There were the text books for the military English, how to get landing lights on, how to clean a plane. The students liked him, you worked through an exercise, then you talked, it wasn't strenuous. And they had their money from Saudi Arabia. Some students showed him photos of holidays in Tunisia with a group of prostitutes, fat girls. There'd be prayers in the college mosque.

It all went on. He was mainly back, though, with the girl. He looked out of the restored window, drizzle crammed its square panes, the trees stood up bare on the muddy slopes, the new tarmac of the drive was set with kerb lights, coming on in the dusk. He was depressed, down, wrote to her, got nothing back. He hardly earned much here. He didn't have a phone and in any case it wouldn't be much use ringing her.

There had been his room in Tehran, the seething streets. This place was this, now the genteel English town spread out bland, tourists came. The Arab was face down in the leaves, it would be good to join him, feel the wet mud on his forehead, smear himself out of the usual. A queer dark was coming across, it seemed to spread up from the base of the hill and in the evenings the asylum begun to reassert; the glossy fire doors and dead retiled entrance area receded. Queer muted cries rose up, they seemed to be in him, deep pains that would not pass. Then, one day, the swathed shape broke free and had rushed into the class, sat down with the landing lights text book open, then begun a rocking and shrieking. The students were moving aside, he was dirty, an aberration of Allah, a couple spat in his direction to insulate themselves from contamination.

It went on. How did you structure it up? With no belief in the extant it was hard. Jobs, who gave a fuck? Who actually could care about the usual scenes? A kind of joy came in the hatred. The best thing was to put his bare head on the earth. That way you could feel the spin, the other motion that broke the English sluggish rotations, the inexcusable wrongness of the systems there.

He could see up ahead, with a sudden shock, a white swathed figure jogging on. It was swerving, in and out of the trees. Sometimes it slipped in the mud and leaf mould and its bandages were smeared with grime. He supposed it wasn't grave bandages but a medical sort. Lately, the college principal had altered his duties: sometimes he was allocated care slots in addition to teaching. At first he'd made mistakes, now he understood more. But perhaps this wasn't his charge, just a swathed shape perhaps from a cemetery come in for a run on the slopes where the old asylum crested the summit. It was like himself, running, kinds of bandages slid over his own body where he had nursed his own condition. You didn't get over it. It was like a rape in a secret zone, people took advantage, made you powerless and you lived on with the feelings. Maybe the Persian girl had been passive in his spiritual rape by her father and his friend. Too much was unexplained, unanswered.

The figure was ducking back, queer eyes looked at him, then it was off, the leaves were splaying up and a kind of lead trailed behind. He made no attempt to follow, restrain. It was like himself running away there. From high up, behind, a small group had emerged at the asylum's door. The figure would be back, run to Heathrow, crammed onto a Saudi airliner, Prince's son, flown home in the restricting bandage. Then he'd be got out, future city, skyscrapers, women swathed, Allah's land, to be shut up in a luxury apartment, shipped back later or who knew, murdered. The English were about, Saudi deals, who cared, fuck everyone up, Iran, sell to Iraq. Was it the most materialistic country on earth, the lowest, England? Allah would burn it straight when judgement came.

People were coming, he moved on down the drive. They'd contain the shape, structure it back to its room, secure it, benign and careful.

He worked on at the college. There were the broken days. You tried things. Some kind of relationships happened but they weren't important. He picked them so they weren't. He could do his other work, maybe rewrite his thesis. A line of contempt ran, for himself, everything. Zohre was at the base. If you failed, you went back to the beginning and rebegan. It was possible to unpick the tangled line that cut you and to roll it out sweeter. At the same time the society ran corrupt, around, another year on.

He got her letter at random. He read it over, pleased, walking in a London park. He'd taken foreign students there, a trip. There was the heat again, the sun was blurring in the distance, new bank towers glittered across paved concrete places, trees poked out. He was walking in a small grove, the sun shining hard in his eyes. He felt one eye go black then a haze of blood was running small across it and there were fragments, he could feel them, below the line of blood. A low branch was whipping back up, hardly visible in the sun glare. It was another thing, he went fast, the hospital wiped his eye clear, he lay back, local anaesthetic.

Now he would recover, and go to her, since she asked. Things receded, it was out front in a clearer state with the pains experienced locked back, you could be Jesus or mad for revenge which was which, or a broken, plunging figure head to the ground for the griefs. The world was full of them, episodes there could be no apology or explanation for, acts of simple evil, social and exigent, personal too. Best to put your forehead in the mud like the swathed figure in white, trailing the bandage that kept you shackled, now torn away. If your eyes bled from the sights and what was done to you, then you could clear them, see clearer too, straighten up.

The train was running south in the heat. Outside the landscape was turning to hot moorland, soon the train would arrive. He'd travelled all night, crossed the Channel by ship. Perhaps a person could achieve, not discover in the end a life had been in vain. He hoped it could be so. He wasn't thinking of her or him. Things seemed suspended, shut up in vegetation and the sun. Nothing much seemed to exist, outside the trajectory. Already the past was a long way back. It would catch up, overtake and be there ahead.

Now he was getting out. She was waiting, had come with a girlfriend. Like him she had gone back in a daze, past was present. She looked thinner than when they'd last been together, more elegant but also nervous. A kind of new fragile poise held her. She was cautious, would estimate, it had been real before but she'd cut it up, her father had told her to. She had existed in her own wound that she extended, made into a labyrinth.

She came forward, kissed him in the French style on the cheeks. She took him in, appraising. He'd stay with a friend, she'd fixed it. She'd take him there. Then the next day they'd meet. So far nothing was explained. He stayed exhausted from the journey. He was always exhausted, had to travel hard to get to her. It was weird, things were silent but everything was announced, they would proceed again. But he felt she would check him out, see how things still were. And this time it was Europe.

He was at her door, knocking. He'd rode out, as she'd instructed, on the bus to the residences, brought breakfast.

She bent forward to let him into her small room, her smooth brown arms clear against the white of her nightdress. For a minute she leaned strongly against him.

'I don't want to make love', she told him. She was smiling. 'Anyway, we know we can do that.' She paused. 'I want to make my mind up without that.'

'Make your mind up about what?'

'About getting married to you.'

In any case she led him to the bed.

'We can sleep, tell each other what we dream of.'

Anyhow, he thought, she knows what making love is like, from before. But why should she take charge, 'deciding' as she put it?

She was taking things up, from where they'd been broken before, back in Tehran. There were no reasons, no explanation, just emotions that ran physically. There'd been the past, even before he went to Tehran, they'd driven from where she was studying and felt everything receded in the heat and bushes with themselves at the centre, their feelings actual. Why, you could be making a career but in fact that only seemed absurd, the impact of the night and heat and her floating in front of him, physical and graspable. She felt like an element and he loved her, in the dark, not so conscious. Now she wanted to try to be reasonable, it seemed against herself. What did you need, to be married?

Maybe it was a question the women worried about more. The conventional answers for some women ran easily round their heads – there'd be the money and a kind of ethos, all the time mixed with consumer excitements, and a man to support you and so it ran on, glib. A woman could be a kind of picture to herself in her own home. The girl, asleep, had rehearsed all this, she knew it, and maybe that he couldn't do these things. Also she couldn't care less. And what crap it was, she wondered too, who put these thoughts, good reflexions, in her head?

He woke up from an uneasy sleep. She was next to him,

half awake. He didn't like this hanging off, the 'deciding' as she put it. She was set back, not as before. Then she had come forward more freely. Something new had been written in her brain that she had to deal with. It seemed to come from outside, maybe she had grown into the risk of it being there.

Now she was looking at him, her head resting on her arm, her breasts part revealed in the white shift.

'You see, I want to be sure if I marry you.' She was laughing too. 'And now I want some coffee.'

He was amused as he walked down the hot corridor to the empty café. It was his role, on these mornings, to go there to get drinks. He liked to wait in the spacious place, out of time, no-one around, no requirement. Partly he was cross with her, partly not, she would do things her way. His way seemed to recede as the days passed and he didn't care. She would follow her own route, it would shape up, in the end.

Only the two years when she hadn't contacted him were a kind of weight. The blood had been wiped off his eye; other kinds of wounds remained. What had she been caught up in at that time? But he didn't care, now was now. And how much did it matter, anyway, this personal life, these feelings? Something else spun, just as real, a hidden turning force that operated as life, snatched you back, pointed you on, killed you in the end, or if you preferred, made you die. Either way, it was a killing, you were gone. And thousands of people went into their feelings, got married – for what kind of meanings, what result, too, collectively? But you could spin with the bigger force, perhaps, could she?

A Frenchman came eventually to serve, there was sometimes too a man from Brazil, he'd come to know vaguely, sat at a table, half asleep. The man didn't seem to know why he was there, just that he had to sit out the summer months as a student until he returned. People always had somewhere to return to. It was wearying. The sun was blinding if you looked through the open door where it scorched white. He wondered, as he waited, what it meant with the woman, why it was happening as it was. He had no control, she did it as she wanted, saw best.

'You see, I have to go back, to Tehran. And there I will ring you, to say yes or no, to give my decision.'

She had rehearsed her procedure. He knew she would do this, she was reliable. She would proceed. But it was an odd thing, to decide in a void, almost without embraces. But it wasn't a void, it was her home. He mistrusted it, after what had happened. Before all was impulsive, extreme, physical. Maybe in her female way she was correcting, trying to be cooler now, do the right thing as she saw it. Only he didn't like how it was. He agreed, knowing the days would pass. He didn't want to lose her again. But also, the locked back feelings disturbed him. She hadn't cared how he felt before, she had abandoned him at her father's wish, given actual wounds, betrayed all his efforts.

Once they drove to a queer, brittle new development by the sea. Brown concrete blocks rose in slabs from white harbourside constructions, boats rocked in chrome, there were shops, all new. French people moved between. Things moved on, newsagents were full of globalisation news, stock market fashions, the new ways.

She walked with him a short way, looked at a clothes shop, not part of it all, or of anything. Heat burnt up from the concrete, slowing them down, making a trance. She was looking at him, now, across a table, a sad, blown to pieces look, fragile poise.

'I wouldn't eat – at home. After you'd gone. They took me to doctors, then I ate again. But it was because I had made my mind up to eat. It was nothing to do with them.' She reached across the table to his hand.

'Now it is better.' She was apologetic as she spoke.

'I remember – coming to your house in Tehran, your father sent me away after that meeting.' He was reminding her.

She looked at him, again in apology.

'He sent me away too, to get over it, to Switzerland.'

Again the man was uneasy. Why hadn't she contacted him?

'He forbade it.'

Some weird force of reasoning ran in her, it was better then to forget, the family would never have agreed.

'So why will your father now consider us – the marriage?'

'He will consider it. And you must do this. Write to him from England – don't say you've seen me – and ask. Then he will ask me. And I will decide.'

He looked at her, could see she was reworking it all. She would go back to the start and come forward. He trusted her. It would be as she said this time. She took control. A price was he would be left out in the process, a little. She had felt dirtied by the first procedure, her father and family had hurt her, made her nothing, just as the man had been. This way she was restored. Also she really wanted to be married, she loved the man, she knew him in many ways. But she wasn't to be exposed.

It was different now. Her land was broken in on, socially broken. It had been broken before, then, in reaction it was broken again, in different ways. She with it had been twisted, sent out, brought back. The hatreds ran in her for the regimes, the King, now the Imams, for her situation, not free, not anything. What was she, what was she to do? She had been powerless all down the line, with her parents, the King's cruelties, now to the religious men she was a western tart fit only for re-education and discipline, always nothing. What did she want? Was it car rides at night, discussions, to give her body up to ecstasies, to walk down a shopping street buying things, to sit in a home, a beautiful place, what else was it to have in conjunction with a man? She had liked the first three things with the Englishman and these things had been taken from her. The other items on the list were outer things, she had her own thoughts and feelings but they ran below the rest.

Then she had given up in some way, no-one paid

attention to her. This man had done his own things, his studies, he had an essence, that existed and she liked it, but she ran strange. She had liked his letters but she didn't reply. There was no place in the world for a woman, you had to do man's things, get a job, get an ambition, she didn't want to. But the subtle things no-one saw, you did them, you fitted yourself in.

She didn't want to be violent or aggressive, to consume, but instead – as she put it to herself – to be, to live. But no-one let you, you were harassed at every turn. And now her own land, in spite of the effort to change, the murders, harassed her in its new form, just as the old form had harassed her with its secret torturings and military, western deals, its queer atmosphere.

The man, he would be her husband, maybe felt the same. He didn't like his own country, it was sick in other ways. Yet she wondered if the man should do the struggling leaving her the space to be – the man would battle with business, like her father, to provide so she could do as she wanted, even if that was nothing. But this man didn't seem like him, he didn't want to battle in those ways. She grinned as she knew this, it was better, together they would turn aside what was extant, maybe overturn it, take their own path.

The sun was glaring harsh on the white metal tables and there was no vegetation to break the heat, the stony new construction context. He was looking at her, trying to work her out. She moved her chair closer, kissed him hard; that side of things was right. But what did that even mean, that side of things? What did you do with a body when all was taken over around you? But hers was stirring, it was there, against him, her spiritual self too. He grasped it, intuitive, the destroyed land, her father. Flags hung limp from the sterns of boats, the heat hung down, bleach white. She was used to the heat. Back in Tehran she would come to her conclusion, she knew it already.

He was thinking, the social realities, conventions, didn't work for him. The chance, the upward movement, careers, wouldn't happen. He was his own reality, didn't care. He loved the woman across the table, whatever it meant, the difficulties involved. What would be created, a life in these conditions? Things were fractured, outside, England's cruel foreign policies, its greed at home too, Iran broken, making itself a pariah zone. It crept inside you, the outside parts, you were not exempt, even were responsible in so far as you didn't resist. Maleness and femaleness were swallowed up, distorted. He wanted to find out what it all was, bring it back, the fiercest contacts, unsocial.

She sat back in her chair with the blue sea behind, her dress clear white in the brightness, her hair dark and glowing. He liked her because she made it possible, this naked contact. They could go on, find things out. Only it would be up to her to avoid the pitfalls, not lapse, once he was gone. The millionaires' power boats rocked behind.

They were back, the road was still hot, the Brazilian was driving. It was his car. He had broken English, nothing to do and drove with them, for them. Why should he care, he was bored. But he liked them too, couldn't say why. He communicated with the man through football anecdotes, particular free kicks, players. Maybe his family had money back in Brazil, maybe not, who could say why he was there, in France, at all. He seemed not sure, himself, switched out in the café, oblivious, waiting for the time to go back, fly in. Sometimes others came to the café, bars, drifted in, Australians, other Iranians, chatting. All were young, there was the future ahead, no-one knew its shape. Days passed, it was time he should go, the girl stood with him on the TGV platform.

He hated to go, she looked at him, would ring, would decide. There had been his departure from Tehran. That was undone, now. But a residue ran on, the past intertwined in. The platform swam in heat, the train waited. She was kissing him again, it was like before, when she had left England. Only there were the wounds since. Something unhappy hung in the air as well as the future; in the distance queer events hung, to be helpless against. At this time it didn't occur to him that there was anything much you couldn't reverse or act upon, you got more experience as time developed, people perhaps worked against you, tried to bring you down. Of course the social whole was against you, he grasped that. He loved her form as she stood by him – that was one mystery, how you could feel so strongly. They would do something with it all.

He wrote the letter to her father. It was acknowledged. She was ringing. It was the new phase, they would be married now, she confirmed it.

The generals sat in a circle. The room swept curved, with a garden and fountains beyond, a queer arc of military triumph also outside, a pointing sculpture, a scrub of deserted land, beyond. In their uniforms the men were the same, visiting advisers, similar, wore suits. It was all carried out in words, it was men meeting, and afterwards it would be put in train, what the words meant. Behind came the pressure of money, weapons to be sold, already sold, backings, the English and Americans were in the room, anonymous helpers. There were hands with hairs and veins pulling out documents, human voices flickered, a landscape of feelings and resolves came about. The men were authoritative, how they were communicated to the world saw to that, what they were was elided.

The jets were up, flying in formation across a mountain range. They'd not come far, just from a neighbour country. Tehran airport lay below, there were the Iranair markings on passenger jets, a tanker refuelling. The pilots were adjusting mechanisms so the bombs would tear up the Persian runways. It was a start, and the international aids, the provision of foreign bombs and equipment supply lines were in place. You shot people and put them in a pit, they didn't bother you again and weapons companies in England and America got contracts.

Where they were bombing they were against the US, England, they'd come out that way. Another country would provide this time the means of western revenge. Arms were all around, you sell them en masse everywhere you could then you maybe swung against your customer after taking billions from him.

Back round the table the fingers with veins inside had tapped on electronic keys for figures, configurations, abstract diagrams had appeared on neat screens, the computers had set up the systems, men had worked on the weapons software accounts, how to buy, and on the intricacies of the weapons themselves. Now it all went down the electric systems from the neat units, clean.

A face loomed to speak the pre-prepared words, all had hearts and organs, walked to a meal in another room, but the message was only abstract, the screen picture. All was for morality and the right, righteousness was American and English and the partner country could not tolerate instability and religious fervour on its borders. The pilots were banking back, the bombs were down, the runway burning, it was over, functional, the war had begun.

Back in England he heard the news. Tehran was bombed, invasions at the border. It was two weeks since her return. The marriage was on. He was to fly out there, in three months, the date her father fixed. An English leader was speaking on the screen. Justified aggression by a neighbour, with significant arms contracts won for the benefit of the UK economy, all advice being given to the neighbour state. UK citizens were advised to keep out of the area. The words came out, abstract, software produce.

Henley was triumphant in the English wood panelled room. He was risen, a high minister now. All around low reading lights gave off a green haze of light. He was pacing and forming policy.

'It's such a boost! We sold to the deposed King, we sold to the neighbour, and now there'll be so much more, billions, consultings, equipment.'

'And we give a kicking to Islam.' The Prime Minister was turning, a grin of triumph lit on his fat, slightly red cheeks. Henley stood tall in a tailored suit.

'Yes, the unshaven ones.' He gave a snigger.

'I can't stand all that open collar stuff.'

The Prime Minister was looking, there was a picture of them both at an event at Eton, wearing tailcoats and a combination of tie and shirt with waistcoat. The King of Iran stood with them, a benefactor. Henley was pointing out.

'Remember that Mohammedan in the Remove!'

Henley was laughing, the Koran was shit, he'd never read a word of it, and Christ was his God, up bleeding on the cross with the wounds. He liked wounds, would imagine them on a body, the broken places where spears had gone in, then the nails. He looked at his own white hands and the suit cuffs. It was Christ's work they were doing, they were helping everyone with the arms sales and they were in the right with their support for the invasion.

'Of course, the collaborative regime is also a suspect one.' An American was cutting in. He was grinning, picking up the tone.

'Yes, we load them with weapons, take the money, get favourable oil deals.'

'And when the time comes – we fuck them over.' The American was endorsing.

'We win all ways round.'

It was just men talking in a room, running the world. A kind of hush was falling at their own importance. The American was smirking, his own President kicked ass overt not like these simpering red-cheeked boys. Vaguely he wondered if the Prime Minister's bottom was like his face, flabby and slightly red, the images were flagging up, there'd be an attack mission across the desert, the American troops would do a storming, Tehran, it was like Spielberg, there'd be triumphs. The Prime Minister preferred British imagery, the American was too fuck-ass in his view.

Suddenly a kind of screechy sob was high in the room. The American was emotional.

'And they've got our boys. Three hundred of them. Locked in the Tehran embassy. The bastards.'

Henley was looking. It was right to have patriotic fervour.

'They're all heroes, everyone. Like our dead boys, our soldier boys, over in Ireland.'

There were pictures on screens, a line of British made tanks were curving along a featureless road with scrubland each side, six thousand miles off. The troops had foreign faces. A few English advisers were visible too, jaunty in turrets.

'Get them out of the picture.' The Prime Minister was uneasy. 'We're fucking covert, covert, covert.' He was smashing a lamp over in emphasis. Henley was soothing, 'On to it at once.' The American sat silent, watching the pictures.

Henley was out of the room, walking fast down a long corridor. Pictures of former military celebrities were on the walls in neat frames and dimly lit. He gave the order to get the advisers out of sight.

Then he was pulled in the direction that came on him at times of crisis. Christ ran in his head as a small boy with a torn shirt, sitting bowed at a lake, thinking out a miracle. There was the wound, like he'd seen in a picture, a black membrane, stretched like skin over a hole in Christ's side. The pictures were accelerating, he was also running with the soldiers to spear the lord, see thick lines of blood run down and he twisted the spear in the wound so a kind of new colour washed in there, a queer liquid of a red or orange colour, shifting to grey.

Better use gas, he was talking. By now he had driven to a familiar street, run down, was walking to a small house to make the call. Then he was back, it was a system he had, to call from there, a routine, his own apartment.

A knock came, it was a workman. But from a heavy box, wheeled in, the workman was grinning as he opened, came a boy, his boy, the young Jesus. Yet he was snapping and spitting. Even so there was his brown body as it would have been in Israel, making the clay bird models live. The boy was hanging to bite and there was the torn shirt, just as he imagined it, it was a sick boy who he would heal himself, Henley. It was charity.

The workman had withdrawn and Henley stood facing the boy who was tethered at the feet and had flecks now of foamy spit across his lips. Suddenly the boy was at him, his lithe brown back slipping through the shirt, biting and Henley was picking up the mask and letting a poison spray off, what they sent with the tanks to use, a lighter dose, the boy was slumping and Henley was poking at him, he'd gassed Christ in his living room and given him fresh wounds.

The workman was packing away.

'We've a different thing on, sir, if you're interested.'

Henley was bland now, the box was sealed up and it had just been a light burst of gas this time, nothing to worry about.

'I would be interested. If it is an experience like this' – he gestured at the box – 'that will assist me to benefit our military interests and economic positives.'

'Yes sir, it may be. And it will help you to gain access to cultural knowledges you may need in future conflicts.'

Henley was thinking. The workman was dressed now as a commander and should be addressed as such. The two men saluted, it was part of an official protocol of provision that was a new development. There would be further events to look forward to, insist on.

Now it was luxuries Henley hankered for. He had his home, he knew, fitted out clear and technological, everything neat and of the highest quality, his cars were pristine, he ate in the finest restaurants. He was stroking down his suit sleeve, the quality was fine, silky. His face had a milky sheen, he was a leader from a further, higher zone. That boy, though! Before the gas he'd had at him, a spear jabbing in his side, the brown flesh torn open. The naval commander had stitched the wound back closed, he was also a military surgeon, used to keeping Henley's cretins in order. They were always tearing. And how good the gas fuck was! He could feel the tingling in the flesh enclosed in his suit trousers still. There came the queer cry, accumulating, like a roar and he was smashing about the room at the military busts, sacrifice was crap, it was himself the world was about, just that, he deserved the best and the group he was in did, and got it. They all got it, he was laughing now, creaming his face, show it all off, he was in with the U.S. president, he'd even met Madonna, he knew drugged bitches, they entertained the troops.

An English leader was speaking on a screen. The rehearsed words were calm, dignified, it was an authority who reassured, who knew the world, who had the best interests and moralities in mind. He must, by dint of having reached high position, be without question deserving of it. The minister didn't really give a fuck about anyone but himself and his own position but that was his secret, trained up as he was to give an opposite impression. He was a master of impressions. An American speaker, as expected, was now on screen, more overtly belligerent, but the US did things differently, everyone knew that, out of an explicit desire for the right to be respected. It was true, too, that the Iran regime was also corrupt and false, like its neighbour, the whole situation spun in an acceleration of falsities and aggressions, all the parties liars and would be profiteers, all claiming to be in the right. This was people, the world.

The younger man was watching. Zohre could be womanly as this raged round her, he could be masculine, but this was their world, the context to exist in. The marriage would happen in it. And the companies were geared up, electronics, war equipment, careerist sellers, products everywhere, there was no place apart. Billions of dollars, pounds, rials swirled about, lubricants, feel them blow, invisible, you bought myriads of deaths. In this world success came or not. In general no-one made remarks about it, it was impolitic to seem outraged. Your leaders chose and you were left with their context.

She was washing when she heard the blasts. Her back was at an angle to the taps, her breasts hung privately, she was for once relaxed, accepting the risks of the future, enjoying the thought of the man. From the window she saw the sun glare intensified by knots of fire and black plumes in the airport direction. She knew it was significant.

In the lounge, her father sat stolid. He supplied the present leaders with 'services' as he put it, as he had done for their predecessor. The blasts might mean an increase in business for him, or not, he could adjust internationally if need be. He would adjust to the winner's side. Yet he was fond of his daughter, watched her as she crossed the room in her bathrobe. She would be married and he could go to England. Up above the noise of a second bank of jets bound for the airport broke in – it was a sort of end.

'Of course, we will be safe here. If there is an invasion it will be on the western border, far away. And our army will hold them off.'

'But it will alter our lives. And, look, they bombed the airport here.'

'Our lives are always altering.' The father was final.

They were silent. It was true. They were breaking up, the times, again, smashing into new forms. She ran off to the bathroom to vomit. Each new form was more disgusting than the last, people showed themselves worse. Everything was muddied over, her father would be worsened and in her way she loved him in spite of it all, he had been kind to her.

Then it was over, and there came cracks from the airport, black oily smoke as aircraft burned. On the television foreign spokesmen were sitting together, abroad, calm, then the screen blurred out and their own channel showed churchmen and jets taking off.

She was back at the new port, in France, with the man, in her mind. How would the marriage incorporate these things? She would like to lash the leaders, their foreign words droned out like products, lies, in some virtual world they chose to inhabit that had relation only to satellite space and a closed upper enclave of the sealed off. You couldn't ignore them, they'd be on you if only in the shape of ideas they spread from London, Washington, which others swallowed. Economy was all and they organised violence. If you were against them, they came with bombs, indirect or direct, it was the same.

He had a dream, caught back in a slum room. He rang Zohre from a basement. The call rang out, there in Tehran. When she answered her tone was low, not as before.

'I have bad feeling. I need to decide again.'

He could feel his emotions rush downwards, in a physical swoop that hurt him. He was agreeing she should take more time, make herself really sure.

'Ring me in a week.' She ended the call like that.

He had a job here, part-time, languages, made the call at night from a basement book storage room with a phone in. It was hard to get through, the line clicked and echoed, there'd be listening in.

'My feeling is still bad. My father tells me I must decide in a month.'

'That's okay, you must wait to be sure.'

But things ran lower. She seemed to be wrapped in herself, he was out of count. It wasn't clear in his dream if he was dreaming, perhaps he was ill, it happened as it seemed to happen. The weeks ran on in a low decline, an unreal mode spread in him, so he himself seemed scarcely real and the black phone down in the basement connected him only with dark things, obsessional. The weeks passed.

He was ringing. She answered, brighter this time.

'I have decided yes. And in two months you will come, we will be married here. So you can be pleased now.'

A queer doubt moved him, now, low.

'Yes, I will come then.'

'And you must bring three thousand pounds.'

'What for?'

'In case we get divorced. It is the custom. And a ring. With diamonds in.'

He knew he had no money so his spirits sank. He had just finished his studies, got his Ph.D. now, had spent all his money on completing that. So the dream went on. In it he couldn't explain to her. She didn't want to understand.

'My sister, Nasrin – she told me not to ask you. But I said I would. It is not much.' But to him it was.

He was looking round at the stacked textbooks. He had no money, earned very little in the part-time post. He would get another job. But why was she asking?

'Ring me later, the line's bad. And I am cold, I am naked here, I just had a shower.' She was encouraging him.

In the dream it went on more. He got a job at a school but could only afford to rent an apartment where mould grew on the bathroom ceiling, a constant damp spread in the rooms and the place was impossible to heat. Yet, in six months, he could begin a better job abroad. It was fixed. They could live in Switzerland, by a lake.

She was asking, he had to buy a wedding dress, two expensive rings, a dress for her smaller sister, come to Tehran to be married. Yet he had no money for these things. He tried to tell her this.

Then in the dream it was war. An army line moved to the Iran border, the English were backing Iraq to invade. Iraq jets bombed Tehran airport. The Iranians kept US hostages, people who had assisted the Shah, in an embassy. He rang her.

'We could be married outside Iran.'
'Then, for my family, it would be wrong. It has to be Tehran. We must agree on these things or how will we agree in future life?'

Somehow his spirits plunged down. The dream was running on. Miserably, each day from the frozen room he went to work. The marriage was three weeks away. Again he phoned her.

'The marriage could be somewhere else.'
'No, I don't like it when you say that.'

He came back from work. There was a parcel with her wedding dress on the doorstep in the rain. He was ringing her on the evening he was meant to leave. Yet he had the money now, borrowed, his ticket too.

'I can't come.'
'Then you are very cruel.'

He spun down, he hadn't gone. The dream went on. Instead the days stretched out blank. There was a little drab wood where a feeble stream pushed through, suburban countryside. He thought he could go in there with a rope and hang himself from a tree. Once he went, just at dusk, to see if he would. The dream trees swayed real and a February drizzle hazed the air, there were cobwebs lit up wet. She was beyond him, the dream had repeated the past, in it his communication with her was destroyed and the war was in full flow. There was gas that sifted out of warheads to paralyse and rot the Iranian troops, the English and US helped provide it to the Iraq army, they were banking on victory. What if the gas seeped here, an hour from London, rolled through the wood. But here was here. He had the wedding dress back in the damp room. Her father had asked if the 'affairs of the hospital' had been completed, the Islamic circumcision, maybe you got inspected for it before the wedding and, if not, were taken in the American limousine to the cutting place. He'd hoped to avoid circumcision.

Or you stepped off the plane and were at once taken to a

basement and chained to a steel pillar in the floor. You never got as far as the family. The English were unpopular. The wedding goods were in your case, left stacked in a warehouse of uncollected or lost cases on the airport perimeter; the white dress lay inside as the planes bombed and you moved on your chain. Maybe these were dream coward thoughts.

He was deft, the rope swung over a branch. But now he was deciding again. He wouldn't do this thing. Rather he'd let the sludge of thoughts and moods take him on, months of it, regrets, wrong decision; he'd not gone, so he'd take the consequences. He pulled the rope down, threw it in the brook. A run of silt backed up round it in the thin water, around. A light mud was on the surface of the footpath, the trees hung thin, the place was half hearted, lost. He'd brought it on himself, not gone.

But also she was the dream-witch who hadn't compromised, who had insisted, who had ignored reality and been willing to run him risks and tasks for no reason but to spoil everything. You could be married anywhere, even near her country, Turkey, Greece. But she had chosen to ignore that and insist on a family event in a warzone. He kind of hated her for that. The dream would end with the months of depressed lack of energy or interest ahead, wondering why she had lapsed back into conservatism that destroyed their chance, their relationship. You could throw three thousand pounds and the rings into the swamp – he'd have preferred that – what did the money have to do with them?

The dream bothered him. He had it again and again. It linked with the image of the white sofa in a luxury room he had when he slept in Tehran as she arranged his flat. What was she used to, what did she require?

There was good news. His thesis was passed. The first one had been failed – he'd written a new one. He was offered a job, out of the blue, at a Swiss University. But these things didn't feed in to her frame of reference. Things were unclear, there was a clog. Maybe it was in him. But her doubts had done it, made him feel she was unconvinced. He was hung back, couldn't see as it was. The more a mood of stress developed, the less it was clear. Then he woke up, the dream ended.

Bigert was reviewing troops, ruler in a neighbouring country, as commander. All was in order. You could send diseases out, no-one cared, something novel to frighten the others. The foreign advisers, Henley too, all said so, would provide and also sell gas weapons, advice. It wasn't clear why it was all happening, some weird international network had ordained it, now it was begun. There was a popping as the first rocket left, it would burst and spray out, they were in for a long haul, not Tehran yet but they'd get there, bound to, with all the backing. He'd spray out gas, shoot one of his ministers at a meeting, he was in the mood.

Her father was supervising, the wedding would be in Tehran. It would defy reason, it would go ahead. He gave out instructions. The groom would become Moslem, complete 'the affairs of he hospital' as he saw it, get circumcised. A mullah would maybe inspect before. At the same time the war grew more intense, no-one foreign went in or out of Iran. The attackers were awash with foreign weapons, a stream of dollars and pounds was coming in, advisers, surveillance from a distance, space satellites, monitorings, tappings. Thousands were being killed in gas attacks down there, over there, in unknown border zones where no-one went, dirty regions of disorder. He was to come, the groom, to have the sugar rubbed through the sheet, to be married.

Bit by bit it dawned on her it was impossible. If he did come he would perhaps be arrested at the airport, maybe thrown in a pit, chained to a radiator or ring cemented to the floor, anything, vanish into thin air as many did, her friend's brothers, an uncle, to be dug up later. Heads might turn up at roadsides in boxes. Also she knew the three thousand pounds marriage money was causing him problems. She couldn't care about it, her father had insisted, a formality, a deposit against divorce.

She would go out herself, back to France, She was decided. She would invent a pretext to convince her father for she needed his permission to be allowed to leave. She would cause a scene, a special wedding dress, other clothes, could only be got abroad. Then she would stay. Or perhaps her father would come himself, in the end. It was all simplifying down, she didn't care anymore about prestige, here, family display, traditions, jobs, money. It was all discredited. In the West, she felt, the same things led up to war machinery, selling weapons, gas equipment, keeping families affluent; England, America, the rest, sold where they liked, now to the attackers because it suited them. The ethos was production and sales, the climax was cruelty everywhere. It wasn't just men, there were career women and in her own land ambitious girls wielded guns in support of the churchmen and she was here at the convergence point. The worlds swirled together like an evil spell. Henley and Tasker led it on their side, here Bigert attacked from the neighbouring country, Khampi led the clerics, who to choose when all were sick? Were those their names, some she made up, she knew, but Henley was one, he'd been on their screens. She'd finally be out of it, she'd leave.

Why not be idyllic, why not imagine? She ran on in her mind, they'd live remote, in France, maybe at a border or intersection point. There was Germany, Switzerland too, What did you need? She phoned him, he'd hoped she would, was waiting for her of her own accord to alter her family plan.

You lived at the bottom, why not? He'd get some kind of job; now he was getting off the train in the small Swiss border town. He could assist, at an institute, it could be all right.

He'd applied for the job, low-key, back home, got it. The apartment was basic, not beautiful, down below was a baker's shop, small supermarket, who cared.

She'd be coming in, Zurich airport, not far off, the next day. Now it was some kind of peace. He sat in the bare room with the windows open in front of him, the sun bleaching in. In the distance peaks rose, he'd had peaks in Tehran, visible through a fume haze with white smirched tops. It was foreign and remote, no English things pressed. What happened here he wasn't part of. He could imagine her in the empty room taking off her skirt. It was what he wanted. He wondered what would happen, how it would be. Why did she want to be with him?

He saw her coming, through the airport barrier. She looked happy but he knew she was broken up also, like he was, put into layers, severances, you were smashed up inside as well as in some places intact, reality had done it. This time she wasn't frozen off or up, she came forward warmly, as he advanced to her. In her recollection would circle different things, the clergymen, the blasts, collusions of powers and sellers, military products experienced at first hand, her family. She didn't want a lovely home, instead a neutral space, anonymous.

The train wound them back to the small town. Here it would begin. Even her father would come round, see what she'd done as right. From the window she could see the lights gleam of a city across the border; the money shuttled there. Now she would undress. It was peace, for the time. But inside she also was crying bitterly, for her father, her lost and broken family, mother and sisters, no longer in Iran, in spite of the new things.

PART THREE

The men were driving, out along the snow-banked boulevard to where the roadway became a grey strip running over bare Iranian land and animals were tethered up. A few shacks began to appear, then more, men moved with scarves and robes, the streets wound off the highway, basic concrete shells with shops in some. The men were laughing, her father's men, some were Zohre's cousins, his too now, they had something in store. It wasn't clear why they were all here; Zohre wouldn't have brought him here, wasn't allowed to, things were split. What happened for the men was more interesting, freer. Now the car swung onto wasteland and in the distance pipes of a refinery were burning red, the air was black hazed above the surface snow.

The men were pushing out, coming from the ring of workmen to join the fluid run of the religious celebrators. You got swept along, could not turn back. He didn't know, it was about what? But no-one was hostile, just he was there, lodged in. It seemed a mindless flow that ran on, like pilgrims on a bridge only they went in circles, round the alleyways and narrow streets.

They came in a rush to join, men in white shirts beating their chests. It was sinister, the bright gleam, the movement slick like pouring in of syrup or oil. Oil ran in pipeways through the edge of the area with shacks, men moved about in pyjamas, mental patients or people with disabilities, let out for the festival.

The men in the white shirts led them now and he moved with the companions until they slipped out of the flow to

THE PERSIAN WEDDING

join people on doorsteps of shops watching as the others ran on. There were flecks and sprays of blood on the white shirt backs as the men began to beat themselves, wounds poked through rips. An atmosphere was developing, they drew curious glances, they should pull out, the festival wasn't for visitors. Men tugged at scarves round their necks above long robes that fell like night gowns.

It was like dancing, his feet were moving and at times he was lifted up off the ground as shoulders pressed on shoulders, some were squeezed up. The men in robes in front were moving one way, then the other, like dancers in a routine coming down stairs and the rest followed. His friends were behind, one in each row. The sky was dark behind the line of concrete shops and the black steam from the refinery fired up beyond, but you could only just see it, the shops closed you in.

Then his friends were ejecting and he was too, leaving the line. He was here with the woman, his wife now, her land, a visit. She'd come from where she was to marry him. Nothing had been going on for him, before he met and loved her. Things had been winding down back then, came to be fruitless, expectations as he finished his Ph.D. emotional, social, that came to nothing. But here he knew nothing, the earlier past was gone. It was better, an unknown place. The men were taking him by the arm, they'd drive back to the city. He saw the glare of the oil processing depot reflect back in the dark glasses of the nearest man, a line of light right up the lens like a crack.

Now the lenses looked back, the landscape was broken into a waste area where the religious crocodile was twisting between a curve in a fat pipe and a distant wall.

'It'll be the cemetery. They're going to have a chant.' A cousin explained.

The car began to bump across towards the burial area, then swung across a flat plain. He felt he couldn't breathe and energy was draining but that he wasn't inside himself. The queer car registrations, symbols he couldn't understand, made him go unreal, he couldn't be understood if he got out here, in the waste place by the graves. He wasn't hardy though in the past, he knew, hippies had come by, another time in buses going to India, maybe unfazed. He could try to be as they had been, cool, but it didn't work, he couldn't. The place bombarded him, the wasteplace mood came at times regardless of outside picture. It was all in the world.

A few people in brown robes were poking at objects on the ground just by the wall to the graves. The robes were of blanket material and one person held up a burnt thing. The man with the lenses was calling.

'It's the gassed, the burnt.' The other men were sombre, had had relatives killed, then they were smiling again. The car swept in under a modern monument built by the king, but used now differently, like a scaled down Eiffel Tower in concrete, and stopped.

Body parts spread out in blackened cylinders, limbs, bits of head, a face with its complexion and surface pitted and swollen, feet in boots. The procession was winding near. A few shapes lay in blankets on the ground. A goat sat eating or was it a person, it was in the distance, perhaps it had got a leg to chew and run off.

The darkness was coming up and flakes of snow began to fall. They'd drive back to the city, they'd joined in here. But what had it been, why had they come? He didn't know what he was doing, no-one explained. He could see a group of men in brown lead a figure out and beat it with sticks in a side avenue of the cemetery, eventually the man lay still in a folded heap. A queer shape stuck up out of the ground, like a woman's shoulders and a head and then a little volley of objects, stones, flung out from the men as the religious line approached, ever snaking nearer. A thin scream was coming and he put his own sunglasses on against the sound and the refinery glare that was pumping red out as the sun set, even as snow fell in loose flakes. He could see the lipsticked face above the ground and the stones flew.

His friend was pursing lips in disapproval.

'It's the justice department. They come here for the ceremonies.' The guest was watching, something emerging, just further on where wooden poles, electric gantries ran cables to the grid. A thin package the size of a person was sliding along the wire pulled by a dancer with a rope. Then there was the hanged man, shown just as light faded. It looked simple and remote since you could do nothing about it. Things existed as facts that you saw and had to see as actual, like someone fallen over in the road waiting for an ambulance. It was one part of a political web. Other countries had different webs and even foreign ones operated across the border, invading as they chose, adjoining zones. The webs were made actual by queer banks of machines, technologies semi-secret in power, money, beliefs, weapons. The list banked up.

Here you could be married too, if you didn't wind up as a foreigner chained to a radiator confessing sins onto video film. Things were shaken up. New emotions ran, no-one knew how to feel parallel to many emotions felt before but now not so relevant. The face poking up from the earth, revealed, was still now with bloody gashes on the forehead and close to her eyes. People had moved away and the dancing column was small at the end of the cemetery and about to turn, dance back to town. He'd be back too, Zohre would know.

She was there, chic in the restaurant, waiting. Below her chador she wore a black skirt that fitted tightly, a white pullover with a fold round neck; as usual her black hair gleamed, part visible below her cowl. He'd come in, the woman stuck in the ground as the dancers swirled nearby, a sense as well of waste ground crossed with the men until the jammed city had replaced spaces of dust, sand with some ethos he didn't grasp. They stayed with her father, an apartment at the centre, in the middle of it all.

Now he was telling her and she was looking back, interested, from out of her own vision, female but also different in other ways, rich, from here. She made him feel stable and warm. He couldn't tell if they were close or very far apart, somehow it struck him as the same if it was either.

'You see, my father is now with the new justice groups. There is new justice for all. Before he had been with the old powers, the King, but he has his family, he had to align again.'

'I thought he did building.'

'Yes, he does do. You know he does, he built those blocks.'

She pointed out of the window to some distant roofs that rose high but looked alien to the man, with the mountain distant behind with snow that looked dirty. There was a polluting haze of exhausts and industrial steam across weird patches of empty land with pools of oil in and concrete frames of the city getting even bigger. It was all there, you felt it in the dark.

'But also he has new ideas.' She went on. 'Like in Washington, there was rent a wreck car rentals, you could start here, but different names, nicer cars, he has so many ideas.'

'And your mother and sisters are in the States?'

She was looking back, sad. 'Yes, it is best for them there. He knows that. And my friends, our friends have all gone, Ali and the architects, Sudabeh, they are abroad, like us usually. It is all broken now.'

'Why does your father stay?'

'He says he wants to help change things. I don't know how.' She was thinking as she spoke, looked him full in the eyes. 'And you and I love each other.'

'Would you know about the buried woman?'

'Yes, we all do. She'd be an adulteress.' Her eyes looked at him again, straying, suggesting distant spaces, vistas, things he'd never seen. He was always surprised that eyes could express so much, her eyes, but he didn't know exactly what they contained, watched. Things were better part unknown.

'We went to bed together. Before we were married. Why weren't you taken and stoned?'

She smiled. 'We were to be married. And, in any case, I wasn't married to someone else. If my father had known I might have been shut away for a time.'

Her father was remote, moving round the city, consulting in ministries; now he was unshaven and wore no tie, thick set and short, ominous. Before the changes he'd done the same, different regime, in smarter clothes, different times. Then she'd had to be home to eat with her family every night by seven. Now she was married she was free. She was remembering before he had been sent away, she'd gone to the younger man's room in the city every day instead of doing her studies. He'd found the city always alien, she knew, queer colours ran into white winter sun and snow on the pavements ground up black with exhaust stains, light he couldn't understand.

'My father likes you now.'

He smiled back. It seemed to be true, and her father's men took him round with them, he was coming to work with them as well. But they were only here for a while, the man and woman, they'd be going back.

'And what he does is wrong.' She took his hand across the table. 'Everything here is so wrong.' She was smiling, tense below. 'But it is my family – their place. And you and I are all right, we have each other now.'

He'd be out, another day with the men, they'd taken him on, he'd see her again, afterwards. She liked the quiet daytime in the apartment, he'd return in the evening. The car was running, her husband inside, this time towards the mountains but still in the city. Some kind of train tracks slewed beside the road, you could get to Turkey, then further on, Germany, the tracks took you to any place. It was a link to use. Or you could swing north, a line ran to Russia, a change of gauge at the border and tracks would take you in the end to Finland or Murmansk. Submarines froze tied up to jetties or moored offshore with reactors bit by bit eating themselves up, self-consuming, until they broke through stored hulls and dropped incandescent to the sea bed. Things were invisible unless you were there to see and you couldn't know about everything: who wanted to know?

The men were pointing to where a grey tarmac drive sloped down into the ground and concrete portals to industrial electric gates stood bleak. The men had dark glasses on and there was music in the car. They liked to show him things and now it was the nuclear complex. A new line of track stretched to a junction at the edge of the complex and he saw below the wires an electric locomotive shunting a single wagon and sealed cask back down the incline. There was the new logo to indicate radioactive material on the back of the truck. You saw them everywhere on the railway systems. Back in England it was normal, nuclear installations were common, trains of waste from power stations and submarines ran unremarked.

Somewhere it met up, Murmansk waste, waste from elsewhere, you could reconstruct it so the incandescence was contained back to productivity, there were plants. The men carried on pointing, they had on zip up jackets like his own, with heavy linings, some had fur and in the pocket knitted hats like rich players wore on substitutes' benches. He was following the line of vision out to where a patch of cleared land was on a curved hill, the railway travelled under. A few shapes ran, it was indistinct.

The car was swinging out of the complex gates. The area was strangely empty, things were new created and clean, not quite understood yet in significance. Freight cars stood idle in sidings, some from Europe, there were European numbers on the under frames. The wheels had turned under the Channel tunnel on night freight trains, ended up here, perhaps, remarshalled en route, maybe in Munich with lights high over the sidings. Some containers had Russian markings. People didn't come this way, just things. What kind of things were they, that had to come, few knew.

One of the brothers was clapping him on the back, he'd been in prison under the old system. Under the new system a different brother was in prison. Things shaped up the same. The brother had explained it all in slow English. The other cousins were architects, involved in the new city and some of the industrial zones. The music was beating up and a man was herding goats round the perimeter of the nuclear area with a scarf round his head fluttering red against the snow. In the distance the shapes on the slopes were more scattered now.

The car was running past palaces where a modern sign had been stuck over the gates and hand written sheets of paper were fixed to walls. The gardens were overgrown and empty boxes with Chinese writing and pictures of televisions on blocked an entrance. From a loudspeaker a tape played over again, a treatise against power and its abuse, against certain alignments, to edify anyone who came to see the bad, past places.

Suddenly they were through, a line of fir trees with the mountains in the distance, you never got closer, then the cleared space on a small plateau, the land rising beyond. Just below and behind them was the high wire perimeter fence of another industrial complex. A few boys were kicking a football on a half-marked pitch and at the far end he noticed a group of men like an official party around the goal posts.

They seemed to be waiting, looking back down the road. One, seeing the architects, waved across, they'd worked together at a ministry. In the distance a line of vans was curving past the plant with black Japanese four by four vehicles at front and rear like in a documentary film about war zones, distant places, evil welling up but using objects that could be anywhere, neutral, ladies driving out for English lunch in the same. The vans turned in at the pitch and he noticed the boys pause in the game.

Red corner flags blew in the icy wind from the mountains now and an elaborate net was set up with extra fittings. Two men with red scarves flapping attended to them. A kind of mute with a gaping mouth had sat down on the pitch and a small group in pyjamas with a keeper from an asylum had assembled. The boys were drifting over and the architects and guest.

Van doors crashed open and guards led out captives. It was to be exercise. A few floodlights spluttered on, directed at the goal as a mobile generator was kicked on and some kind of address, through a loudspeaker, was taking place to men pulled from the vans. Addresses were formatted and on tape, scrapy like a tin voice. He noticed with a shock that the vans had been the King's, taken over by the regime, military, made in England, torture cars.

The men were led to the goal and ropes that suspended from the crossbar fastened round their necks. There was no dance or parade, as at a festive stoning. The ropes were round and then the guards from behind raised the men from the ground by pulling the rope over a pulley, at a signal.

Some of the bearded men who had been waiting for the

vans were having a kick about on the pitch, the ball curved as they passed to each other, one was receiving the ball and heading it back to the feet. The ball spun off, ran to where the architects were and the guest curled it back. They were calling out, Beck-ham, Beck-ham, then came a whistle and the men were pulling the captives up tight till their feet were off the ground. They wound the ropes to secure them to piping that weighted the goal net to the ground. Some of the captives had eyes that bulged then seemed to burst, then had a final, dead knowledge in. The last consciousness hung in their eyes, a couple looked surprised as if it hadn't been what they imagined. Light was starting to dwindle away and the figures hung, swaying.

One of the men who'd been waiting ran over, it was a joke, he'd put the ball on the penalty spot. Then they were taking them, penalties, the ball was flying, cracking the faces of the swinging men, hitting them in the groin, til blood ran. Others ran with sticks to obliterate the faces at the end of the session beating the eyes and mouths unrecognisable. The lunatics had drifted away before and the boys had gone back to the opposite goal mouth to go on with their game.

A few old women, all enrobed in black, stood stern and close, eyes almost covered in a curve of material. A small boy might run three miles to return a school book in an adjoining village to a friend, try to find him, not succeed, run elsewhere, help, kindness could exist. A film had shown it. The men were climbing into cars now. The hanged men with obliterated faces swayed slightly on the ropes, the architects and their guest were also moving off. No-one was speaking, they'd been roped in, one started, made to watch and if we hadn't it would have been noted, there'd be some outcome or effect, something.

The car moved off the darkened pitch, queer red hung in the sky, there was an inflamed moon that came when pollution was up. The women would be waiting for them, in skirts with warm bodies, wives, something apart from the cold grassed area but not making up for it or offering explanations, in some other zone of luxury, different realisations, priorities. He didn't know, the guest, if he and Zohre were different or met up, somewhere, became the same. Things used to seem more similar, sympathies and thoughts, on a par: now they flew apart, even sex didn't synthesise. Should she see the same things that he saw? It was a problem. But they were close, even in the differences, she hated the hangings and violations, she clung to him closer in their bed, at the centre.

There was some kind of block ahead, a sign shaped like a fish swung outside the lower storey of a series of cubes, one storey built on top of another. Sometimes they'd crash, people would lie in the rubble, an arm in striped pyjamas stuck out. These were building accidents but lately it happened, other kinds, explosions, a mix went wrong, random terrors.

The line curved round the edge of town. He saw the tracks lean, seventy years ago in another war the English locomotives had steamed round with rakes of fuel trucks for the British navy ships. Made in Swindon, the locomotives ran here, Iran, for the English and the fuel was annexed, owned and pumped out by English companies. Now it was different but there were still armies about. The woman had said her father had some mission here, further on, supplies to bring, things to fix. The car travelled further and further. It was another trip.

You crossed or you hadn't, the war zone border was wild and it wasn't clear when you'd gone over. Maybe someone came out with a gun but you didn't know who, what he lined up with, there were a lot of groups. Nor could you say what each wanted, maybe it was a mad thing like running the world or having priests put in place to do it, but at the same time having everything, having controls, being able to point and have someone's face broken. There was a rush to discriminate, make distinctions, marginalise, put one group beyond the pale, get elevated. You could blow someone up if you didn't approve of them, have it done back to you.

This time no-one ran out. There wasn't much to see, space, a few rocks poked out of yellow earth. Zohre's father was down below, talking to someone, the black car and driver waiting. She stood next to her husband, looking out at the sparse zone. They were married now, she reminded herself, pleased her father hadn't minded in the end and there could be an advantage for him, a line out to somewhere else. He'd minded in the past, before the troubles, forbidden it all, but now it was allowed as everything else had broken up, like when you trod on hard dust and it just broke up, choking you. You never knew here, how it would go, you could have your leg blown off and still go on, it was the zone, or else be on a bed on wheels with blood on your stomach and a drip, rushed with shouting into a ward, where some people just lay, bandages where limbs were torn off.

Instead his daughter could go somewhere else. Things were relative, the father had no final commitments, belief was gone. She'd had enough, wanted to go. Now the girl and man sat in the back of the car. She took his arm, tight, stayed close. The father was in too, front seat, they moved off across the tarmac through the dust.

It was exhausting, no-one spoke, the drive back would be eight hours. In the distance a speck grew into the nuclear train, twin locomotives and two wagons with flasks for the facility. They'd be heading for the complex. The world ran luxurious in the car and the apartments back in the capital yet the front line was receding in, no-one knew clearly where it was, in some cases it invisibly ran in the city streets themselves, surveillance was high, even in space where no-one could breathe or survive. What went on wasn't known in detail by ordinary people, technology was remote and strange.

The girl was leaning against him, he knew and felt she was his wife, he was convinced of her worth but he didn't know why he was here in this different place that was precarious and temporary. It would well out and be everything, or else become nothing, the mode here. It would end, in any case as a Mullah said, when you were dead. It was dark, she and her father were asleep, the driver drove on, red lights on the tips of a landing plane, passengers from somewhere else, it was random, could be Moscow, Helsinki, you could get anywhere, come from there.

Zohre was waking up, the nuclear facility was on their left, they were passing. She clutched his hand, kissed him.

'Let's go to London.' She looked at him, a little pleading.

'Why there?'

'Why not? We met quite near there.' She was remembering the bushes and flowers in the heat, walking in the dark. It seemed far back, a few years, things changed, another lifetime, coming in from a wilderness. What had he come in from? Some kind of zone of pain, it struck him; that was how it was, projects crushed. She'd made him happy. Where she'd been, come from, was alien even as her familiar home city, she'd not known herself there. She had been happy in the English wood, in the sun, with him.

'We can go – see it again.' He was smiling. 'And maybe other places too.'

'Let's go – quickly.' The places seemed a long way off to her. The car was in the black, turning up a road of villas, low luxurious apartments. They lived here with her father. It was accepted, the son in law was part of the group.

Now they were lying in their room asleep, shapes only below the cover, somewhere else. She woke up, he felt her stir.

'Yes, I want to leave.' She was definite. 'We'll go and do other things.'

'What sort?'

'We'll live somewhere and you can work too, like you did before. Like when we were in Switzerland.'

She wanted to be stable, settled in a rhythm. This place was jarring her with its breakages, there were splits, trouble leaked out everywhere or showed itself blatant and unapologising.

'It sounds peaceful.' He wanted it too, there should be relief, here cut into you, filled your head with hard sights. Once he dreamed of all the injuries he'd seen, in miniature, maimed people lay small in glass bottles with tiny pools of blood and body parts. Then, huge, he saw the face of the stoned woman, imploring, in the ground. Some kind of trauma would unfold, if he wasn't careful, that would last forever. She looked at him in the half dark, kissed him again.

'We'll go.'

Sometimes before, they had gone out, there were restaurants they went to. She was exotic to him, this place was far off, he was different here, at times set free. It was strange how in the chaos these moments came. She was smiling in the shadowed place. He was remembering.

'We came here before. The first time you were here.'

'Then you said your father had to decide.'

She looked down.

'Things are different now.' She was smiling. 'But it is still the same feeling.'

'What?'

'You are the best thing that happened.'

He smiled back. It was odd, they could be happy, in the centre of it all.

There were other things to say.

'We are always moving round.'

'I don't mind – that's how it is. And next we go to England.'

'What will your father do?'

'He has some "last things" he says to complete. Then he will travel himself.'

A waiter was bringing food. They felt remote, happy in their own world.

There was one trip left for him before they could depart.

The men were laughing. They liked to have the guest with them, show him things. Outside the complex one was asking.

'We can have nuclear things, why not?'

'Yeah, I don't see why not. England and America have them.'

'And what's Iran done? Nothing. Just defended ourselves against an invasion those countries supported. They go around doing harm.'

The guest was nodding.

'And their nuclear fleets cruise under the sea. They come here, the Gulf.'

The guest had seen the submarines, deceptively small, moored at Devonport, the nuclear flasks travelled from Plymouth on the railway to Sellafield, reprocessing fuel.

'Only they can have them. Because only they know what's right.'

Once a high Mullah, a minister, had visited his wife's father. He sat in the apartment in the city centre. He liked to talk to the guest.

'You know, everyone hates us and our country. And things are not perfect here. But at least we keep our disorder mostly inside. Whereas your country exports violence and at the same time poses itself as a moral arbiter.' The guest knew this to be true.

'Yeah, morality is a big ostensible thing over there.'

'It's like a dress, for show only.'

They were laughing. The English guest was speaking more.

'You know, I like your version of the crucifixion. It wasn't Christ who was on the cross but a substitute. God took his messenger back unharmed.'

'Yes, it's so morbid, the wounds, the suffering. Yet you in the West like to inflict these things.' The Mullah was curious.

'And Mohammed had wives, wealth. He enjoyed himself.' The guest was endorsing, Jesus was miserable in comparison, that was certain.

The Mullah liked to discuss. They would pass on to philosophy and even literature.

'Kierkegaard believed in redemption, you could go back and begin again, past time becomes future time, you redeem the past.' The Englishman was interested in the possibility of such change.

'Yes, redemption is not so possible in Islam. Especially for the non-Islamic, they might burn as sinners. But then they make weapons and wage wars. They go on and on, they are not contrite. But if a believer is contrite he can extricate himself. No one else's blood is involved.' The Mullah enjoyed explaining finer points, as he saw them. 'Of course, there are different interpretations to mine.'

'Your adulterers cannot redeem themselves.'

The Mullah was thinking.

'No – Islam is wrong in many ways.' The father was looking on, he also liked now to discuss. He was shaken, his family was abroad, his wife and other daughters, the wars had made him reflect, things were troubled, on and on. There seemed no end ahead. He was waning, he couldn't enthuse anymore.

'So why do we go on with it so strongly?' The father wanted to know.

The Mullah looked back.

'Not all of us want to. We can see it is unintelligent in many ways just as Christianity is stupid, often, but it's what there is, we use it as we like. So we go on from there. It shaped up, a learned holy man returned to us, a few years back, an interpreter of the old truths, he became leader. Now he's dead we go on in his spirit.'

'But it doesn't make much sense.' The guest spoke.

'Nothing does. Does England make sense? All goods and services at home and blood abroad, tortures, secret things the English at home must never see in any full way, or at home know, how the machines work, the death directed vileness.'

The guest was wondering. If nothing made sense then how could marriage? In what context was love happening? The Mullah was watching, perceptive.

'You are thinking of your wife. Take her away from here. This is no place for her.' He smiled across at the older father. 'And take him too, sometimes, into your home abroad.'

He was turning to the guest again.

'You were telling me, how your writer, Lawrence, endorsed before he died Dostoevsky's indictment of the Christian, the Inquisitor's conclusive accusation. It is too hard, to be a Christian and it leaves the material thing in the hands of the satanic.'

The guest was responding.

'Some truth. England and the US are surely satanic. And Lawrence said that, too. That production, selling, families based on that, leads to a mad, violent evil, a consummation in destruction, atomising.'

'We know that. Yet, we produce too, obsessively. But it's all like children, throwing insults, we call some others Satan, they call us backward devils. All is true.'

There was a pause. The Mullah continued.

'Maybe it's true, too, turn the other cheek, take the blow, kiss the giver. What if America had suddenly forgiven terrorists? Think how the wind would be taken from Islam's sails. The believers would be non-plussed. Instead the US came running, with England, guns blazing, wild west, colonial wars, revisits, sometimes oblique, but with advance weaponry, fortunes spent, like people with disabled brains let loose. Whereas, how higher, not to react, to be above reaction, to replace attack with good deeds.'

'Does Iran do this?'

'Not at the moment. But we do far less harm than those other powers. They spend trillions on nuclear submarines, weapons, and say we may not. Of course no-one should have nuclear weapons. I am a man of peace.'

'But not in your current role.'

The Mullah closed his eyes.

'It will come. All this will fade, the stonings, it will all come to stop. Who knows when? It is all false, here, the West too. The world will be different.'

The father was looking, eager.

'When? Everything is wrong.'

'We do not know. Do we need yet more messengers to come to tell us? I agree, as Dostoevsky said, never will they be able to share, never will they understand higher values, turn cheeks, reflect in silence, focus themselves, see beauty where it is. Instead they will squabble as the vile and slaughter each other. A pity Dostoevsky didn't write also about Islam. The fields of fire, never be friends with an Infidel, shame on you, only Islam counts, burn the satanic unbelievers! Of course if the latter attack you, you should burn. But who understands the messages? People can't do it. I can't, I wait for it all to end. I'm tired of messages, messengers.'

'When?'

'When I'm dead. It will end for me then.'

Outside the city was quiet, the windows were black. The men were silent. The guest could hear the voice of his wife talking on the phone to her sister and mother in California. He couldn't understand what she was saying. There would be the boulevard, cars, people in bathing gear.

The Mullah stood up. They were all sad.

'Go back to Europe. Take your wife. One day I will visit you, we will remember what we said, see how things are.' He had the guest in a close embrace, like a hug, for a moment, spoke,

'We are both believers.'

The Mullah laughed, – 'What in?' – swung his cape over his shoulder, looked back, left the building.

They were on the last trip. Along the quay frozen water stood jagged, up in diagonals, and a low, grey sky ran as horizon. Hulks of craft were jammed together, snow frozen deep on decks. They rose, ominous and huge, out to where a thin line of ice broken water cut white. Already it was getting dark in the early afternoon. The brothers stood on the quayside, in black overcoats and scarves, chic wool hats and the guest stood with them. It wasn't clear if it was a job or not, they'd just brought him along, a flight to Moscow, another flight, train and car, to here, this limit, Russian coast near Murmansk.

Queer grey black hulls stood frozen over, further out than the rest of the discarded fleet, there was a metal watchtower lined up amongst the warehouses behind. The men were walking, it was hard to keep balance on the frozen street that was broken at the edges above the sea-ice. Weird gleams of white shone out and in places smoke rose off the water surface, misting objects over.

The men would be making arrangements, a cousin had told him, they'd gone inside one of the warehouses, Victorian red-brick, rising out of white, to do a job. The guest was waiting outside the door, looking north to where the ice compressed and gathered, had a focus. A queer flurry of dry snow was blowing circular in a frozen breeze.

No-one else was about, the reactor in a submarine had, a few days back, eaten through its shell and fallen hot to the sea bed, plumes of steam rising, there could be other accidents. Bodies in a cemetery were discovered preserved in peat below a night sky of flashing blue, it was a feature of the town, or the moon stood huge, ten times its usual size, amplified in pollution. Some kind of tracks ended just short of the quay, there was shunting, the short train with flasks. The brothers were coming out now, slapping him on the back, an experience, he'd done well to come, they were amused at how he adapted.

'The first time I came', a cousin was telling him, 'I saw on that mill chimney the temperature: minus thirty-five.'

'It's the same now.' They were laughing, last night they'd had hot opium on a golden dish indented round the side up in a flat with oriental carpets on the floor, outside the windows was pitch black sky and white ice crystals, snow. Now the apartment blocks built basic for workers poked up concrete, and the train was idling, loud, across the deserted road. A few lights flashed on loading vehicles. The men were climbing in the car that would take them south now, then the planes.

Behind, the sea was vanishing into blackness and a few hazy lights glowed weak on thin standards along the road, like in a pauper zone. It was receding, the wooden slatted houses stood in carelessly laid squares on wasteground, the place was running down and there was a bleached area where some device had spilled chemicals out.

The guest waited briefly in the dark, the men would pick him up at a road junction. He'd been sent ahead in a separate car. His wife would be back at home in Tehran. When he got there, they'd leave. He was relieved. He didn't know why he'd come – her father had insisted – except to see the place. And the father wanted to show him what he did, how his business worked. The guest knew, the father wanted to give it up, it had no meaning for him, he had told the mullah so. Yet still it went on. An icy wind blew in from the frozen sea.

The guest was somewhere else. A plane had taken them now to where a queer casino stood by an Iranian inland sea with the railway line passing near. Their freight would go through later, intact, they'd checked – it was a regular shipment, the flasks were solid, it was government to government and in the north you were closer to units to reprocess the fuel if you wanted or to get new supplies.

It was good it was backward, this area. It was discreet, you shunted stuff about, weren't conspicuous or in a hurry. So now, below the roulette wheels, a radioactive fuel train was passing, there was material. The brothers had shown him how far in they were, the systems and so had the girl's father, while she studied and was in the flat in her own capital. Sometimes a churchman had smoked opium with the brothers and other deals came their way.

They'd showed him the deaths again too, stoned torsoes in the sand. Once he'd seen in a room men chained to thick pipes that ran along walls in the dark. Other men came to hit them across the head with heavy spanners and there was a small side room, like a toilet on a French campsite, old style, with tiles on the floor where a man could lie, curled up while he was kicked in the face and head and blood ran down a chipped drain. We copy the English army, a man had explained. The brothers had wanted to tell him there were possibilities. It was hard to know their alignment. Now in the elegant room with soft carpets, they were relaxing.

The roulette wheels spun from time to time and a dirty sea lay flat below the window. It was half hearted, lassitude only. His wife's father was coming in, the black coat like they all wore being taken off his back by a casino official. The father came over, shaking hands, at once the leader, given deference. The brothers were standing up until he sat and he was smiling. He turned to the son in law.

'So you have seen, you know our projects. And you can be useful too when you leave with your wife. We will contact you, over there.' He looked tired again. It wasn't clear if he meant for a job or for his retirement. The older man nodded towards the west through the windows, backlit now with a queer glare where the sun set.

'Or rather there', he moved his arm northwest, 'the quickest way, Russia, Berlin. I was in Berlin, Hamburg, for studies. We will be in touch. And your wife is packing, what cases!'

'Yes, you will be really welcome. And we are off, very soon now.' The guest spoke, concerned. The father would want to stop his work, had passed beyond policy, caring. It was best to be quiet, peaceful.

Outside another train was passing, a reverse working to the north, just three trucks and a locomotive, more flasks. In sidings longer freights were waiting, there were Russian and Chinese markings on containers as well as languages from Europe. A haze of grey exhausts spun over the locomotives as they waited with their freights. From time to time the roulette wheels turned but no-one was keen. Men met here to talk things over, relax after deals were done or successes achieved. You could fly up from the capital. In the distance oil field chimneys funnelled more haze.

It was queer, the guest felt out of time, poised up here between his own departure soon, where he'd just been and what went on elsewhere. It was a verge, a literal frontier. Across the border you could run on tracks back. Objects come daily from places he knew, in the containers, on the rails. Other things went out. But people didn't come this way as a rule. There were strange conduits running secret across huge areas. Elsewhere it was packaged, how you went, what you saw.

The older man was rising, the car would drive him to the capital, he'd sleep, he preferred it to the rise and fall of the plane. The brothers and guest would follow on, sleeping in turn. In a day's time he'd leave, his wife with him.

There were city sights, a huge arch built by the king. Now churchmen milled under the modernist structure, it was a place for permanent dissent. There were big sheets written on, changed each day, and bearded men stood ominous beside these. Sometimes there was an address and exhortation to keep pure, not relapse to the old ways. The car passed and the scene was gone, his wife was beside him, her father in front, next to his driver. The scenes were endless; at a junction goats grazed and the signs pointed to the stoning grounds.

Ahead the lights of the airport cut in the haze and beyond mountains glimmered with snow peaks through the grey. He looked at his wife, she was holding his hand in the back of the car. They didn't say much, understood perhaps by look and touch. He wasn't sure sometimes what was understood. It was strange, she might never come here again, he might not return again either, this departure was unusual, final. The father was turning round nodding, he'd be in touch, there'd be instructions.

The glass doors slid aside, automatic, as they stepped from the car through the cut of cold air into the terminal. Inside churchmen clustered at a counter, they were grinning, eyed at the father. He was shaking hands, they were smiling at the departing couple, there were links abroad, changes, something oblique was going on he didn't understand. He was part of it or not, he didn't know, his wife didn't care, just wanted finally to depart. The father was grinning, there was calling out, 'Murmansk', laughing in reminder. The dark Mullah he had discussed with was smiling with the rest, calling out, 'Best thing – to go', and they were through. Other zones en route you skirted in the air in case of missile attacks, the Americans had shot an Iranian airliner down, Europe was just six hours off. You were out, could feed back in there. The churchmen were laughing, it pleased them, the new scenes, connections meant services came back in, imaginings, adding to their ways, gratifications, revenges.

She was leaning against him in the plane, it lifted off, they were together, still alive.

PART FOUR

For once it was hot. They sat in an English garden where bushes ran at the edge and in a wild part nearby birds sang as the sun burned. The place belonged to him, there was a small house. Things were transfigured, peaceful, here in the countryside. She sat back in her chair, her legs slightly apart, her white dress loose.

'So, we have come here now. What shall we do?'

'We have our jobs fixed in France – for later.'

'Yes, the teaching.' She looked at him. 'But now it is a kind of holiday?' She was asking, turned to him.

'Maybe your father will come – until then we can explore.'

She looked pleased. She didn't know what to expect. Things were mixed, they had gone through the contexts, different places, harsh and sweet experience, all. Sometimes she wondered how it was, things spread out in her memory, there were different colours, things ran red like blood, there was the vivid touch between, imaginings flowed together sometimes, joining them.

Now the sun was beating stronger, he had the shades on, she was standing up. Clothes were a continuity, he'd dressed like that when he sat with the Mullah, his jeans had been in Tehran, on his body, now he was here. And she had worn the same dress to drive with him, her husband, to the border zone, his hand had caressed her. He got up too, moved to kiss her. They'd move soon, maybe in a couple of days, go back to the capital, start the holiday. He'd fixed it, made arrangements.

*

THE PERSIAN WEDDING

They came in, it was the city all around. Another organisation was here, England, secular. They wouldn't pick up her father til later or maybe not at all. A queer empty feeling came, nothing specific to do. She had her father's money, cards in her bag, her husband was on the payroll too. But for what, it was unclear. Anyway, they'd be freed up.

They were in the station terminal. He knew everything as if he hadn't been away for a few years, she was remembering too. Now being with the foreign family receded, it was like being put down to start again. True, they'd been left to themselves, over in Tehran, but had been referred over and over, back to her father, relatives, contacts. He'd liked it, partly.

There'd been the sights, stonings, amputations, the nuclear trip north. It was like being mad and then enclosed in soft comforts; horrors were outside but then you sat inside in an expensive chair in a luxury room. Not different to London, just a new external of the vile and in any case here some horrors were kept at the distance of several countries away. Though England had its own, close up, too, injustices were rife.

She was half asleep, now, in the chain café. He saw she was both tense and lazy all at once. They had to wait, it wasn't time yet to go to the hotel room they'd booked. The hotel loomed, over the station, another brand. This was it, paying for things, a main English mode, the empty English feeling was coming on. Only their feeling for each other countered it.

'Of course we will have to pray.' She was smiling at him, neither of them much cared about religious forms.

'Where? Down on our knees, heads down on the station floor?'

A queer cooler wind blew into the café entrance, things were going grey. Armed police were making a circuit, glanced in at the café but English style discreet, take it in at a look, heavy hand in reserve, and in any case, the matt black of guns across chests.

'Pray' had been picked up by the word recognition

devices installed here and there about the station and its facilities and the words flashed on surveillance screens in a room where people monitored. It often threw something up. There were many enemies, people who prayed were suspect, and although ordinary life, lower, went on it was as something just allowed and artificially maintained. Another real life, money, weapons, went on hidden, parallel, higher life.

She was asleep again and he saw vaguely on a screen on the wall opposite the constant news, a fat man in a suit entered a bank's door and reporters were calling out 'Are you embarrassed, Sir', and words ran below the screen, 'Prince involved with sex offender', there were pictures, arms sales, him having tea with Arabian kings, entertaining back home a leader who'd put thousands to death, pictures of naked parties in America with a tycoon.

The Prince had strode on, his bottoms like footballs in the grey material of his trousers as the flap at the back of his coat rose up over his bulk. A hard, thin, woman was with him, adviser, PR, legal expert, procurer, pimp, detective, who knew. They'd brazen it out, carry on the same, this was England after all.

The man was back. The outlets glittered round the station, rustic soups, Mexican rolls, pretend French patisseries, it was toy town. She leaned against him, he enjoyed the sense of her body there. But what did it mean, enjoy? His feeling for her went so much further, appreciation, respect, need. And you were meant to enjoy one of the rolls in brown bags, his mind was wandering, sold by an immigrant in a kind of baker's uniform. Enjoyment was the ethos, the men with guns, the English Prince, endorsed it. Better get on your knees and pray than buy a roll. He was tired, things were mixed up and lost, travel lagged into some stumbling tiredness, he couldn't concentrate.

Men ran, sudden, the concourse was filling with a queer hanging cloud and the blast was blowing a hole in the roof on the opposite station side to where the café was. You could see it tear. She was awake, jerking, clutching his arm. They couldn't see through the cloud of burning debris that hung and the sound blast was still bouncing from beam to beam inside the roof, ringing the rafters with a queer, abstract rhythm. Then there came cries, quite feeble at first, then louder. Just across from her, on the paving stones, was a torn off hand that seemed to grab as it slid from the blast zone, just by itself.

A hand had waved from the ground, a burial alive back where they'd come from, was it the same hand, she was thinking, the one I'd seen. She'd come across it, they'd been driving, rounded a bend and there'd been the punishment unit, the person was just buried in the flat plain and they'd left the hand out as a sign and warning. Now the hand was back, it had slid towards her here. Should she hold it, she was wondering, give it comfort. It lay still, there on the slabs, still bleeding and pieces of shredded flesh – maybe from birds, or was it people – were floating down now, gently like a kind of light snow. Or was it like cremation ash, he'd seen it scattered, his parents, at the cemetery site. It was falling.

He wanted to move but they were shocked into sitting on. Again the impulse came, to bend his forehead to the ground to make the gesture to the non human. The Mullahs had influenced him. From people you never knew what was to come.

It was all wearisome. They were recovering now, vision and hearing returned, each could see the other, lightly covered with still smouldering flakes of ash and grey powdered dust, thrown out of the roof.

'What are we – covered in this stuff?' Zohre was trying to joke, stop shaking, moved to kiss him full on the mouth, kiss the dead ash off his face. In fact she loved him very much, knew what he had put up with to marry her and just now she shared with him the sense of being entirely lost and alienated in two worlds, his own and hers. So what they made would come out of this fact, she knew it. Soldiers were gesturing, they should get out of the station.

Henley stood, some kind of driver, high in an observation post in the side roof of the station. From there he could see everything, chaos on the concourse. A queer grin came. He was the cause. His own men had done it. There'd been signs and he had got his own men involved, infiltrating, encouraging, they were instigators. Without his men there'd be nothing. How it kept him all above, in charge! And the threats made an excuse for heavier hands, 'blow ups like this', as he put it, 'justify us keeping a harder watch.'

He was looking ahead and planning, as from a mast top observing rig, His superiors, and there weren't many, would follow it all, as facts. You keep things insecure, then you impose the order that suits you. The old days had been good, back at the start, when he could set his groups going to give people from Pakistan abuse and kickings.

Yet last night ... He was drifting off, smoke wiped across the window of his rig, he was relaxing. First he'd been over at the screens of the Communications Unit, out in the west. Then his provider had taken him 'just to see sir' to a dingy house in a terrace, a corner shop near Paki places but an Iranian invested. And then, what shags!

There'd been his boy, the usual, the brain damaged one with a brownie's body, couldn't speak. Then there'd been girls, a new thing, twelve years old or so – he'd just watched, not his taste to do, they'd do anything for a phone or a bag of chips, English losers from a centre or care home, he couldn't mind his provider explained. The men handed them round. He wouldn't have anything physical with the girls, didn't like it that they could talk, weren't subnormal. He'd just keep with his boy, dirty and dark, dumb.

His provider had eyed him.

'We take them on sir, the children, of course for you, it's surveillance, the great must have relaxes, that's true.'

Henley had gestured him to quiet but this was the ring,

foreigners were involved, he had a hold over them, if they caused trouble, threatened to expose, he'd run them in, terrorist plotters or have a rendition. His spirits rose, smother them in cloths, then fly off to a base abroad, maybe leave them battered in a rolled up rug on some deserted high road where no-one went, keeping things secure, that's all it was.

It was better than Shakespeare said, to be a king. 'He ruled, he ruled', he was seeing himself. He'd rise up, no-one above, take things the new route. There'd be a group, the richest were with him and low people endorsed, they liked to see success rewarded. How easy it was! And now, this at the station – above and enclosed in security glass, he saw the sights, panoptic. Then he'd be on screen, deploring foreign militants. True, so far he could only risk organising a few such events a year but who knew, more could be possible.

He was itching, another war, good for the economy, you put it across, keeping safe, probably Iran directly next. He dined with weapons chiefs, BAE, Rolls Royce, they all came in and now the government ran the banks and mint he could roll out cash like juices. 'Already am', he was laughing, where did the quantitative easing money go – the term was like what the young girls had done, tugged at your penis till you eased all over them, loose and easy, oily like Mohammed's blob, he was amused – he was already there! Nuclear war heads, rocket propulsions, computer drones, military softwares, pour the money in, spend on surveillance, so much more, massive outlays, for him, Henley, his group, to rule.

They were out of the station and into the London street. The impulse was to walk away. The street was as usual, it offered nothing, just a life of work, a banal norm. Here were hotels, tourists came. One had blown himself up in his room preparing a cheap device a few years back. It was all futile, things were as they were. There was a dirty park with a cold wind blowing across black green grass, a monument to a queen's husband, it was a sight. It poked up, old, dragging everything back, wrong pasts.

Zohre wanted to get to a hotel. They had to find an alternative to the booked one. Inside the room was as usual, dead like the street.

'What did we come for?' She was discouraged.

'To have different things to over there. And to help your father, perhaps.'

'Help him, how?'

'He's not told us yet. Maybe he wants to rest.'

She looked at the man out of tired eyes as he spoke. It struck her that things had followed them, the same, to this place. She spoke perfect English, had studied here, but she saw her words, now, come visual in the script of her own language, translated, in colours, in her imagination. Things were mixed, the jet lag, the country garden, there were security horns now in the area, the dirty lake in the park opposite was troubling.

She closed her eyes, was asleep. He joined her on the bed, lay looking round the room. There was the long wood unit opposite, a wall length mirror. People seemed to flicker in, who'd been here before. They'd been intent, perhaps, business, sightseers, who knew? A lost feeling came, his body was going down a notch in energy and inclination. Things were organised, they had jobs fixed, an institute, France, he'd start in a month. They'd be provided for, things would shape up. His wife was still asleep beside him.

The television was on. A constant line of news ran in. Nothing was much done about items shown. On screen black men hit each other with sticks, one was weighted down with tyres and set fire to. Elsewhere weapons had been identified, approaching a border zone, use against the British, then destroyed by rockets from a drone. It looked like where he'd come from.

Across another border you grew opium in a field and then supplied the world with heroin. It was your life, out in the fields, hitting slaves with sticks if you wanted, ethnic time. He could see, he was passing in the dust road, the hotel spun thousands of miles off from the swathed men, trials in a chicken hut, the Imam sombre, giving a verdict; absolute conclusion from vague, ancient words, holy law.

Against this was the law of going to work, scientific reportage and paying for everything. It mounted up to climaxes of bizarre weaponry and practices. British boys ran in to shoot up the foreign court, the bullets skipped in the dust, you could radio for the drone to burn up a village, piss on a prisoner with his head in a bag. Back in Birmingham heroin was easy, on the streets, time to time, see you through the bad times, the military even ran it in.

Yeah, they'd made the chickens skip, the dust spun in the sun, the snow on the bleak mountains shone lurid white, unnatural in desert air, the men had on combat clothes, gear, radios, guns, computers slung on, come for right. After, the Imam lay jerking on the ground, near him a few chickens twitched to death, the dream spun on as he slept. News was creeping in, now, explosion at a London station, there were breaking headlines and visual shots.

All the time he was aware of Zohre next to him, her

warm shape, being alive with him. Sometimes it was all they had, this closeness. Maybe you wanted friends, a fixed life. Sometimes they had that, it ran in blocks of time, just now they were alone with each other. She was waking up, smiled at him. She was thinking.

'France will be hot. Like when you came there.'

'Yeah, things will level off. We do the teaching, lie in the sun.'

'Not that simple.'

'No, probably not.'

She was laughing, looked at him long, and slow.

'And we will see my family again.'

Things were improving, they saw clear ahead.

They got off the train. It was the middle of nowhere, a long way west. From the platform a narrow road curved into a deserted distance. Why not move, get out from the great centres. She had asked him this. It was still a kind of holiday, before the jobs began. Now they stood, her clutching his arm smiling. So far her father hadn't contacted her, they were alone. She liked it, this freer air.

A line of sea ran at the edge of the horizon. Below a strip of sand lay thin; scrubby land stretched between them and it. The road hung empty across the space. They'd got a key, they'd hired a place.

You could walk, there wouldn't be snipers in these marshes. On the edge of the sea a few houses stood. One would be theirs. They could move on or not as they chose. Things looked empty, no-one was about. The sea hummed at the edge of the sand, a few waves broke, there was nothing.

'What's on the far side of the sea?'

'America.'

She grinned. 'So we've linked it all up.'

They looked into the distance. A grey murk hung across the horizon, misty drizzle. The place was far off, invisible. But if you went, you'd get there, the streets and organisations would be actual, you'd be among them. She shivered and moved closer to him.

'We're just people.' She was thinking as she spoke. Far off, as here, systems were locked on, money funnelled in, more money than you could imagine. What was a billion exactly, most people didn't know, was it a million millions or was it a thousand millions, there were different views, and what was a trillion, that was a million times a million million, you could buy a lot of system with that. But of course you fucked it about electronically, it perhaps didn't exist as physical if it was money, or some did, stored in bullion chambers, or it was on electronic data, in bonds, hedgings, wherever it was it was a web, a maze. And between them England and America had blown trillions away, spent it on death. She was telling him.

'The systems work on our behalf.' He was sarcastic.

'So it's said.' She was joking too. 'Here as there.'

She was recalling the droning of the Imam. He had a rule for everything, for every circumstance. There was guidance available. There'd been kings too, who also had rules that ran in part conjunction with the Imam's system. The sea was shuddering in the distance, a moving, undulating expanse of space. There were facts about it, humans couldn't live in it, its mode wasn't favourable to you, you couldn't breathe or eat in there, the main part. The surface was ominous, risky, but in the bulk heaving below all was hostile to you. It was natural, but laws, systems, were another thing even if they had the same effect, man-made.

She'd had a King, he'd locked up the Imams, then been replaced by them. But the King hadn't been real, he'd been put in place by the same powers that now fought all round her land. History was confusing.

She remembered, many had been pleased when he was driven out and the tall bearded Imam had been flown in on a French airliner. All was to be different, tortures stopped. Somehow it hadn't worked out. A tacit rule operated, wherever you were, people had to be coerced to obey. Here you were coerced by money, the need to have it, to pay. Or it could be, elsewhere, through religious books. And you couldn't debate the text, even where it ran in contradictions, obscurities, as that was done for you by experts. Here, too, it was fundamental, experts made decisions and you fitted in with them, were coerced. Only the decisions emanated from scientific books, secular Korans. And behind it all was money, even the holy books needed oil revenues to have power.

She laughed. He looked at her, pleased.

'We can stay here a few days, move on.'

'Yes, wander round, see how things are. And we could go back to where we first met, just to see it.' She was excited. She wanted to move the drabber thoughts aside.

'And we can see where my parents lived. Go back to that garden.'

She was sad, she hadn't met his parents, just seen photographs. They were dead when she had met him. But she could see the places associated with them, know them that way. She was cheering up. She'd like it, in the garden, in the sun. They'd go again.

They both knew, too that some kind of summons from her family could come anytime. Her father would be devising a plan. Probably he already had it clear but was holding off to give the younger people a free chance to explore, establish themselves, before informing them of their duties. She didn't know what to make of it. She loved her father but his activities seemed oblique to her. She hadn't paid much attention when she was younger, just knew he paid for her, the family, luxurious. And now it seemed so convoluted and embedded, it was hard to extricate a clear profile.

'When will we be called on?'

He was looking at her as they walked on the beach. A queer spray was blowing off the Welsh sea as if the water was spitting on them to go and a hard wind blew in grey, bleak streaks, flattening the waves, from the U.S.A.

'It could be any time. My father will just ring us. We've already sent him some information he wanted.' She looked across the waves, pointing to a line of oil tankers moving towards a refinery round a headland. They were miles off the mainland, tiny at times, part hidden in the dip of the swell, spray clouds. It was another system, you walked on the beach here, out there, on the ships, the electronics were humming, having to be cooled, in the computer navigation rooms men watched screens, the ships guided themselves once the programmes were set. They'd come out of the Gulf, some from her home, others not. Crews might be hired in, an alien nationality took the ship to the export port, then out again, it was global work, often languageless. The instructions were electronic and bodied out that way. It wasn't clear who owned the ships, responsibilities were kept loose and murky.

She was joking again.

'Crude oil darling.' Her jokes didn't always succeed. She looked deeply at him and he laughed. It was crude enough how things were. Sophisticated systems encircled a kind of prevailing baseness, the lowest behaviours.

The wind was getting up, harsher. They moved back off the beach, crossed an empty grey road that fronted the sea. The place was village size, sand blew off the beach in swirls, ran along road gutters; they opened up an ugly house, vanished inside.

There was the entry prayer to say, then the prayer series, you went head down to the ground, you faced Mecca, then you rose. Then his plane took off. It was the north again, the frozen place. This time the father would go himself. It was organising and he liked to be hands on, have a change in Europe. Something was afoot, ordinary people wouldn't know about it. Then he was giving up, retiring.

The car swept along a causeway where a frozen river was set in swoops of ice and a high sun lit everything up in detail. There were to be the new explorations. But he wasn't here for oil. A border zone opened up, there were pine trees and shacks. It was a special barbecue, there was salmon from Lapland cooking over a fire on a griddle and a black limousine drawn up. They would agree, the men. A dome of some kind of energy plant poked through pines at a distance and a small stream lay frozen rigid in a ditch.

'And – as usual – we continue as before.' The men spoke in English. It was confirmation and they drank the vodka to celebrate before starting the fish. An odd glow was in the sky, it was getting dark, mid-afternoon, the pines hung up skeleton shapes against the darkening blue. The two men spoke more in English; behind, discreet in the trees were the security officials. It was covert, like molesting someone, an international arrangement, you used railways to move things, special road vehicles went obscure routes. People might know, after all there were spies and technical watching devices even in space, people weren't told in general, they had rough ideas only.

THE PERSIAN WEDDING

The father looked upwards as if, high up, he could spot the turning canister with its aerial wings, transmitters in space itself. A vast space writhed above in currents and swirls and then you got airless and far out metal rolled monitoring. Who watched who? It was universal mistrusts. Maybe the English and Americans could pick out words, hear them via space, they were devils.

The men hadn't much in common. There was some banter about fishing in remote lakes and rods to fit the occasion. The counterpart was taken with the topicality of rods. He was laughing, tapping the father lightly on his thin stomach. The father was laughing too. It was like back in his orchard when he'd been younger and he'd made jokes. Then too they'd let out girls and caressed them in bushes. But here it was too cold, and in any case now he was older it wasn't so interesting though there'd be times he'd be in the mood. And his wife was in the States.

It was light talk.

'Russian girls. Some went over the border.' The Russian pointed across dense pines vaguely to the west. 'They got to a village in Finland. There was nothing there, a derelict farm, a shop, another farm, a few houses. They set up in the farm and the men came, Swedes, Finns. They made a lot of money.' He was laughing.

'Yes, yes, in Iran the men go out. They'd run anywhere for women. They go mad for them. Abroad is best.' The father was remembering. The story was surely true. The Russian girls had astounded the regional authorities but couldn't be dislodged. The northern men had used them, exotic destination, like a remote fishing trip. But the anecdote bored him. What was the point of it?

The men were getting back in the cars. The system was already set up, this was habitual, an occasional re-confirming, cordial and tedious.

'Come, yes, come.' The Russian was beckoning and the father had known a further trip was on the cards. The cars pulled up at the edge of a low, flat, marshy area where a few warehouses stood, Victorian style, incongruous now in the waste zone, different epoch. A track curved to a small industrial harbour. A ship was backed into a dock, not large, but with reinforced bows to break ice. Next to it was a tanker the father knew would head back to the Gulf. It would pass the English coast west. He thought of his daughter, there with her husband. He would see them soon.

The northern sea stretched ahead, flat calm, queer it was, top of the world. Then the smaller ship was nudging on. They were on deck. Up ahead were the drilling platforms, a few slabs of ice floated at the legs of the installations but otherwise the sea was clear. The Russian was laughing.

'You see we put down flags on the sea bed. To show it was ours. And the Finns – how they protested! But they can do nothing!'

The Iranian father was laughing, he pulled his black coat tight around. He was gaunt and urbane.

'So – you have oil here. And rods close by.' He gestured back to where the naval base was a few miles east of the small harbour they'd left.

'Don't worry. Those rods are heading south in one of our freight trains. But now – our oil. And you may help us get it out, your Mullahs!'

The icebreaker was curving round with a slight list as it circled the platforms, it was sight-seeing.

'We can run our interests together. The Imam will be informed.'

The Russian was laughing again, which Imam, we Russians have our own, Kremlin style. The Iranian was still, the Russians blew up Moslems all around their borders, the Imam knew, but still here was a provider, it was the rods. A slow weariness was coming over him, he wasn't young, when would the deals end, the resistances, forbiddings. It wore him out. There was the sceptical Mullah, his friend, his son in law's friend too. Like him, the father didn't believe anymore, politics were broken, dirt on the ground.

'Now let's go fuck those Russian girls!' The icebreaker was completing its circle, turning fast at a list, settling straight. The Russian looked ahead, anticipating. The waters lay flat around, now it was like a wide river estuary, not like a sea, low islands lay emptily at intervals with marine structures on, metal numerals, tripods. A queer black girder, lattice steel, stuck up as a warning of rocks, like a marker in a cemetery only tall and in the sea. The father watched it pass, the water stirred, icy, morbid. It troubled him to see it.

He'd watch the girls too, see them strip off, have them serve him food, it was protocol. Who knew, he might have a fuck too. But he was getting older, even so he could go ahead, you could take a drug, though he didn't need one. It was nothing, you pressed on to a climax, you repeated yourself, it was pointless, depressing, like hammering at broken things. The women were worse, foisting themselves on you, convinced you must want them. All for money and the hammering on, body on body, then nothing, no aftermath. And he'd like to know what men wouldn't, they all had secrets, every man, sexual things, things they'd thought of. There were the things they'd done or seen, even the holiest, closed cars, remote vineyards, city apartments, palaces, the men did things all unadmitted, clandestine. The women too, all pressing to the climax, then nothing, void. Who knew what our needs are, he was running through his prayers in a side cabin, he was plunging down with his head and forehead to touch the metal floor, cold like a torture unit back home, let's go fuck the Russian girls. They'd go across the border, get stuck in.

Iran was far back. In the cabin he was remembering. They were moored up now, back at the dock. The prayers were over and now some other feeling was replacing them. The rods would be en route, swinging on the bogie wagons down the tracks. It was unexceptional, nuclear materials were moved from place to place daily. It was business. The loads would be switched, train to train as usual. And now there was some oil deal up and coming.

But the Russian was knocking, it was time to make the transmission, the Imam would be expecting it. A queer central cabin ran with banks of screens and computers. The line had been raised by technicians, there came a rush of Persian, the Imam was having a joke. The father could hear him exhale, a fume of cigarette smoke down the line, it sounded like he'd put his feet up on the table in his special residence. There was congratulatory remarking, confirmation all was correct, then the line was blank, the screens were closed down. It had been pointless but protocol. And anyway, nothing important was said electronically anymore, there'd be listeners, the internet was insecure and obsolete.

Even the Pope must relax, the father thought. The Imam wasn't like him. Yet who ran Islam? There was no-one in overall charge. A sudden glimmer of goats rushing across a desert area came, he was a small boy, it had been the King who ran things then. What was the difference? It was all drumming in his head but you had to make a living and bring up your girls. And now he was the minister who arranged all, but secret, behind the scenes, arms run out too to help fight the British. Yet he enjoyed London and would visit there soon. Russia was dirty, not so unlike Iran, but London was different, the rich were made at home there and, if the Imam wanted, he could be welcomed in and allowed to buy a mansion in the home counties, perhaps next to a footballer.

They watched the games, over in Tehran, and the Imam had his favourite teams and players. The Revolutionary Guards were familiar with English football grounds, went round muttering them, wrong pronunciation. It was sick, things levelled out, became each other in corruption. Idly the father wondered if Jesus or Mohammed would have watched the games. Mohammed had no holy powers, except for the writing of the Book. Jesus had done miracles but written nothing. What they taught had led where – to this? It wasn't their fault, men made them less, there was nothing holy about mortal men. It made you laugh, and the queer turning of the ice water round the base of the lattice arm, the black metal reaching like a memorial towards the low sky warned him now, he felt, something badly wrong.

The trip was boring him, it went on slow, he wanted to be free of it. The girls didn't interest him. Of course the Book was a miracle. It was queer, he had glimpsed everything was incomprehensible and lost; what he did, the father, was like an oblique substitute for something else that should be done instead. It was all trivial, the rods, the rulings, he was perhaps a low criminal and would never enter Paradise. Yet, here on earth, he was high, at least in Iran. But it was all insecure, he could be weeded out, on a whim. It was a system of sadism, arbitrary. It was the same, England, America, huge weaponry could be poured down by them anywhere, their systems were kept locked also in injustice, unfair practice. Times were backward. In London he could perhaps walk unknown, along the roads, or else spied on and tracked, who knew? And, in fact, it was clandestine, he hadn't told anyone, he was winding down. The rods had become a bore, the process just went on, mechanical for him.

The Russian and the Iranian were laughing. Of course they were winding down. The flasks were en route, in trains.

'But they think it's in the ship. They'll watch it, follow it, back to the Gulf.' The Russian gestured to the large cargo craft pulling out of the dock.

'And we've loaded it. Entirely innocent. They'll waste their time.'

The father was grinning, when it came to it, it was England and America who were the main nuclear threats. And hadn't they, recently, caused more carnage abroad than Iran ever had? They had sided with Iran's enemy in the great invasion. Now the British submarines nosed in the Gulf, their missiles crammed with nuclear explosives. Why should Iranians not defend themselves?

The ship was nudging out, the lights spread in the dark water, colours, the exhausts were pluming up in the icy air. The men watched it go. It curved to the west, slow, making huge way in its bulk, the bows cutting the freezing water.

Henley was following on, getting reports. He was up, in manic mode. He'd been down for a few weeks, something to struggle with, things inside himself, a sort of fear. He'd had the boy, that had been a sop, but incomplete. There'd been no cure for himself. He was black down. The brain damage of the boy was consolation, dumb and queer, like a lithe brute he fondled and had control over when the service provider released him.

He'd never been to the girls again, not even to watch. But he kept an eye on the network; it was intersticed, kept unclear if they – his group – ran it or it was run for them, it lead to observations, a network from Pakistan, potential to blame, you could follow in, frame them as bombers, perverts.

Now he was up, accelerating, watching. The ship would be coming near. It was all drawn up, there was a threat, it was nuclear materials on board, the time was come for a striking. The Prime Minister had been advised, homeland security.

'So we blow.' He was talking to himself, the control centre was in place, train disguise, down from the weapon makers in the Midlands, a new thing, you go mobile, Lenin's train, check back every detail of a firing. It was research too and he was all for science, you got what you did.

The ship was off the west Welsh coast, the jets were up, Henley was waiting, a start, there'd been too much talk, hangings back, he wanted to make a gesture.

Suddenly it was there on the screen, they were in the covert unit, debris on the water. It looked queer, the team couldn't work it out. Things were floating, tiny. It looked like thousands and thousands of wooden Russian dolls, tiny, were spilt from containers and were floating in the sea with sections of the submerged, broken ship.

'What is it then, just toys?' The surveillance team were looking queerly around. 'We blew up a ship full of toys?'

Henley was staring. The flesh began to pull back above his teeth, a cutting anger was coming up, like when he stuck up his boy with tape and powered at him when his limbs were restricted. Sometimes even the provider was surprised as he stood discreet in an adjacent chamber. It was odd, he was a keeper but it was a military role also, and it was strange what the gentlemen like to see and do.

The surveillance team were muttering.

'Yeah, but we can say there was evidence of nuclear equipment. It was heavy and just sank.'

'There wasn't anything like that.'

'Who's to know?'

Henley was above things, the gossip was nothing. Of course the ship crew were dead, whoever they were, Russians, Iranians perhaps, the ship had come from there, goods for Iran, for definite, plots. He was calling out.

'It's started! Started! We'll follow on, strike whenever we please. Fuck them from Hormuz!'

The surveillance team were clapping. The news about the dolls didn't bother Henley, they could see that. One was holding a phone out.

'Prime Minister for you.'

Henley was up, on to it.

'It needed to be done.'

'But with missiles from the air?' The Prime Minister was ironic, drawling, it was just facts.

'Protecting the homeland.' He liked the American turn.

'Quite right.'

Henley had the phone down, was up. There'd be international interviews. Yet it was the right, he had it on his side. True, the crew were killed, no-one could survive the blast to the ship bridge and crew quarters, the missiles had blown the ship in two. And they'd controlled them from the land, from the covert train. All the pilot had to do was fly, they could programme as the planes flew.

'Reprisals, sir?'

Henley couldn't give a fuck. Let them come, he'd smash them, and if the ordinary were killed or maimed it was a price for the right. Rather he welcomed it, the inburst of friction, killings on his own doorstep, better to bring it in than have the killing zones so far off. And it was research too, it appealed to him, there was an academic point, bomb software, that took him back, student days, maths and physics. He'd loved his subjects, he was awash with sentiment, recalls and gushes, and maths had led to the banks' prospering. True, they'd overreached, the maths, scientific debt schemes, software shifts, had ruined them but it was all a worthy price. And others, not the doers or beneficiaries had paid, his group had got off. As they should, the words blurted out, almost aloud.

'The right, the right', he was calling out about morals and Jesus, the swathed boy, thinking by a lake, Galilee, he was tender, the words soothed him, he saw the boy, it was him, Henley, in his youth, he was gentle and mild and then he ran with war wounds on the cross. The figure was looming, the wounds caked over, a queer look, Jesus through the blood, it was swelling up. You jab a lance in the side and it heals over, gossamer, with black stuff webbed up inside. It was his dream. Then he was Him, at the controls, blowing up a station, killings, his autistic boy was the Lord too, you could brutalise, over and over.

Now he stood alone, Henley, looking out of a window on the command train at the sea, with a naval ship in the distance, booming up a space round the wreck, wouldn't want pollution.

More news was coming in, they'd blast Iranian oil ships in the Channel in a few days, submarine missiles were ready in Hormuz, he'd started the cleansing.

The surveillance team were looking, 'Fuck, he's mad', but the new order was coming in, the final clean.

The man and the woman were down by the docks. Ships stood up huge, moored offshore, waiting to move in, offload oil. A Persian flag hung small off the stern of one, she could see it vague, or maybe she imagined it. Yet there was surely the Iranian script round the edging. Now it was here, waiting in line, other flags flew, Russian, Arabic. Behind her grass behind a wall expanded upwards into an extent of heath. The small house was a walk away across a headland. They'd gone up the hill once, a gale blowing, you could hardly walk back, the wind blew the air out of your lungs. It was queer how things change. The ship was now lifting anchor, she saw the jerky, mechanical pull, things from below were fixed to the chains, came up, sludges of green, a dirty puff of exhaust showed at the funnels.

'Looking at the ships, love?' Two men were approaching, one led a guard dog. 'Restricted area. You'll have to move.' The couple turned to walk back, through a gap in the mesh fence. It was a mess here, there was nothing obvious for security to protect, broken pallets, heaps of cardboard, broken containers. The ships were far off, the refinery a mile away with its own pristine limits and codes. The oil had come in, many lands sent it, her own was forbidden. She had imagined the flag. Or maybe Iran's oil came in clandestine, sold on, shipped in foreign vessels, cargoes transferred, not to be traced, she didn't know. Once England had the oil for free, fifty years back.

The guards were talking. 'She's an immi-tart. And he's

brought her in. They're nothing, low lifes. Too bad we're busy today, we could pull them in.'

'Yeah, special job on. Leave them for now.'

They felt lost, he took the girl's hand. Around the heath stretched out. He could see the path ahead but he felt he was nowhere. Now a shoot of flame was up from the refinery chimney far below to the left. A ship lay flat below spread like a diagram. Sheep were turning heads towards them, about to run. He was from nowhere now and it was zero, he was inside nothing. She was walking next to him and that was all there was. He appreciated her black hair and movement. But all was unsteady, there'd been the lines of horrors, neither forgot.

The sea ran flat ahead where the headland ended, a neutral grey band. It just existed. If you looked you made it into something, otherwise it was there just the same. Of course it was true, it was people who did the horrors, chose to, buryings alive, blowings up, but also below the sea's surface were unknown spaces; swimming a mile out to sea you couldn't survive, cold, sucked down, breathless, there were natural dangers. There were nuclear weapons sent circulating in craft below the surface to come up anywhere, England sent them, to turn the world white and to ash. In each age someone came direct from God and you did what they said, Tehran had this official view, he didn't. In London a different thing was believed, you did that. Cause and effect were meant to rule God out, science was causes and effects.

She didn't speak. In the lost territory they went on, she was thinking. She didn't care now, social things had all fallen short, imploded, blown up, there was no background. And now, this future thing! She looked about, a faint sun lit the grass, lightened the grey rim of the sea, the sheep kept turned towards them at a distance, then ran further on. The footpath led to the rented house in the small resort. That much was clear. But inside it all she was nowhere, only with him. It was queer, they depended on each other, she valued him very much.

THE PERSIAN WEDDING

Their heads were down on the ground, they were praying, there in the small seaside house. It was in a terrace, pebbledash outside walls. Inside, storage heaters gave out a weak heat though it was summer. The place felt damp. Through the front window he could see the water beyond the beach, dirty with low white crests now tangled in an increasing wind. She rose too from the prayer. It wasn't Islamic, it belonged to nowhere.

Suddenly in the distance were dots of planes, he noticed it with a shock, heard the far off whine of jet engines. It was an area the English trained war pilots in. There was a base to practise where a wide stretch of beach sand had been fenced off for miles; the jets flew very low across the water and along the beach, it was low flight practise, then spun off into the mountains inland. Now they saw the jets miles out to sea. There'd been wars, millions gassed, invasions, nothing was changed. So now the man and woman went head down, knocked the floor to acknowledge some power beyond.

'Is there one?' He looked at her.

'Maybe. So meanwhile we may as well make some acknowledgement.'

He agreed with this. Why not, it might make something, even themselves, better.

They were walking, leaving now, back down the lane that led across the marshes to the junction station. Things were lit up, one minute bright in intense sun, then the grey clouds blew in off the sea and long dark shapes moved fast above the flatlands, cloud shadows. It was confusing. The jets were still spinning, far off across the headland. She was smiling now, took his hand.

'If you want to be lost, marry an Iranian!' They turned to each other there in the lane, held each other very close. She was laughing.

'And – what is my father. Just what is he exactly?'

The man shrugged, no-one knew, least of all himself. The band of brothers had included him, it was family, that was all. The clerics saw him as a family member, had treated him as that.

A queer smoke, sudden, was pluming up from the horizon, out at sea. It looked strange, more significant than was usual. Deep red billowed in the centre of black, folding over on itself in sinister and destructive glowings. It was too far off to make much out.

They walked on. Across the flat, scrubby field was the small, remote station. Drawn up in a loop siding was a long, dirty yellow painted unit. He recognised it, eight coaches, two power cars, a version of a high speed train, ageing now but revamped and re-engined, that ran the western routes. Yet these windows were blacked out, they were approaching nearer, you could barely see through.

Now he could make it out, one carriage had seats, some stripped out, the next had a bank of equipment, computer screens, technicians monitoring, flows and moving lights. He wasn't meant to be looking in, someone had appeared to move him on.

'It's track testing. But the men can't be disturbed, they don't like to be watched as they work.'

The track testing train was down from Derby, ran in partnership with Rolls Royce engineering, weapons and vehicles UK. There was nothing unusual, it went regularly from place to place. A few vans were pulled up in the station yard, usual markings, logistics, maintenance. But the place seemed over-intent, tense. Briefly he could see on a screen a relayed picture back from above, something white speeding across, explosive. Vaguely he connected it to the planes, the plume of smoke, some disaster. Surely it would be unwise to blow a ship out of the water so close. But it could be an exercise the railwaymen had tuned in to. The blind was snapped down, men were ushering him and the girl away. Things didn't add up. But they'd get away, were leaving, moving on. They'd go to his place, inland, a hundred miles off. They were rising up, happier. In any case in a few days they were off to France. She looked forward to it. They'd work and be together.

They were walking, they were up the lane, All around the bushes swung out, a small stream ran flat, down from the hill. The lane was beginning to turn and rise, narrowing with the hedges pressing in, Trees interlaced across above them as they climbed the acute rise, there were breaks in the hedges sometimes, they looked in, there were sheep, horses with blankets across their backs, wide feet, shaggy lower legs.

She had her hand on his arm, They'd seen the house he'd been brought up in, she was touched. Anyway, he owned it now. They'd leave it alone. She was looking around. They stood on a rise, high now, the lane curved ahead. She saw more hills opposite, flat land long between, the town below.

A queer saucer shaped building stood out garish, on the outskirts. Beyond the air was hazed, another town in the distance, a wide flat strip of water headed remote to a nuclear power plant and the sea.

'What's that place?' She was pointing to the saucer shape.

'Surveillance Headquarters.' He didn't want to think of it.

'Did they sink the ship from there?'

'Probably. Also from the logistics train we saw.'

She was pausing. She'd described the area to her father on the phone, he'd added more details, they'd been laughing. The lane was darkening, it wasn't summer, a narrow strip lay ahead, steep, before the roadway petered out to a track. An atmosphere hung about, down here had come an army to attack the King's strongholds, English revolution. It had been dark, many had fallen, didn't know the route, the cannons dragged behind had overrun and crushed the brutish men. Now all was clear, there was no recall here, the trees curved over the lane as they had back then, the place was cleaned over.

She was leaning against him as she had in the past, in another wood where they had first met. This was different, things had proceeded since, but it was also the same, her touch. He felt older, more things had loaded on, but he loved it most, his arm round her curved body, the sense of her spirit there, coming through.

She was looking at him.

'So we heard from my father.'

'Yeah, some friends of his may drop by later, to the house. And we'll see him too, maybe here, maybe elsewhere.'

'That's good, he leaves us free, we're not part of what he does.'

They were glad to head away. He'd got something definite to do, over in France, low key post, flexible. They had their life together. Now they were walking up the steep hill. Things had receded.

'He is still my father, though.' The girl was thinking. She spoke after a pause. 'It was so wrong, he turned you away that first time.'

The man saw small tears come, held her closer. It was hard to get rid of pain, maybe it couldn't be done, you always had it.

It all seemed far off, border zones, trips to the north, frozen sea, freight trains, even London was misted over, cut back from them, a far-off area. Yet the explosion had been close, then the ship had been blown out of the water too, further over west. She was with him, it was a purpose.

'Look, it really is a bit like when we met, at first.' The bushes pushed out into the lane, there were flowers in the high verges, sun fell briefly, hot. She was smiling, took his hand, went on. 'And later we can go to France, my sister has a place there. For summer holidays. And my little sister is grown up now. We will see her there too. Then work.'

Down below a queer round building, huge, spun round a space like a landed thing. It could rotate, take things in. Then there were the hills, the distant estuary gleamed.

A queer clatter began to come from a low wood ahead. A kind of eccentric entourage was coming into view. There were microphones like sponges, cameras, men holding on. Henley was striding out, in walking gear. It was a documentary on his life, an electioneering piece.

The Englishman could hear him, pointing to the intelligence base below. Henley would combine the filmed walk with political remark. The entourage was past, a few military jets came low flying round a hill promontory, for the programme. Henley engineered the images. He was gone, they heard him descend.

Now it all fell quiet. They recognised the politician.

'Some shit for a programme.'

'Aren't they all!' She was contemptuous.

The entourage clattered down. The couple could see them diminish below.

Suddenly, behind a tree, he saw a black swathed figure. There seemed to be several, below now, three hundred yards down. Another group crouched behind a huge metal storage container for cattle's water, a kind of glimmer was on the matt black handles slung round necks. The entourage were in the lane below, the couple had moved above to where the land sloped rough and down, a few sheep pulled the grass. The men were focused, now, in formations and the shots crammed the silence with breaks and cracks, grenades were slung, there was Henley, face down in the lane and the sponge mikes were in a messed heap across him, camera crew and commentators were also falling, lying on the tarmac of the lane, a line of blood was seeping across to run into the side stream that was adjacent.

Then it was silent. They heard the slam of car doors and

the swathed men were gone. The military jets were far off, it had been just for the programme, they flew round the hill edge, just as Henley came out of the wood, co-ordinated image.

Through the shrubs of a copse the couple could see the slaughter site. They headed off, to descend, another track, he knew the routes.

They were looking at each other.

'Maybe your father's men?'

'Could have been.'

'And good those others are dead.'

'Very good.'

A queer silence hung about the slope. Something smoked up from the site, a kind of haze grenade had been left to smoke out a thick smog around. Where they were was clear. A few sheep ran aside as they approached. Down below a main road curved, bland and over familiar. Cars ran on suburban business. It was queer how war penetrated to here, yet it was here the surveillance centre was, England, the USA, Henley's base. Then miles to the north and east, lay the frozen sea and rotting nuclear submarines, fly south east for six hours, direct from the hill, and you got to where the stonings and hangings went on, there were people in all the places. It was all disgusting, the English comforts and buying things, Americans the same. Always a negative power, reaching to lay waste, destroy, kill and have.

She was walking on, her black hair shone rich but she was unhappy for the time, the deaths had made her go down deep. She loved the man more now. And she looked across at him, she saw he was depressed, flat with the events. They'd go away, go somewhere else. It was queer, he had a house, they wouldn't live in it, things were being destroyed all around.

'They blew up the ship. Bombed the station. Waged wars.'

She was nodding.

'So, they are dead now.'

'Yeah, that's right. But nothing will stop.' It was hard to

think of the carnage, to know too it was just a small proportion of other deaths, daily dealt out, not usually so close to here.

There were the horns, the lane was filling with security vehicles, they were far off now, the couple walked a different track. They'd get out, it was good her father's men had done the killing, they were agreed, it was a step on to balance things up.

It was hot. The table was set out on the beach, the restaurant seats were around, wicker arm chairs with cushions. They saw it as they approached, round the rim of the sea. It was evening, she moved elegant in a white dress, her black hair glittered in the fading sun. He walked beside her, wearing jeans and the shades he'd used to block out the stoning sights. He kept them, he liked continuities. Now they moved easily, relaxed. She was pregnant too. She'd told him as they walked – the heat held them in their pleasure, things ran calm.

Her father sat below, waiting. He was smiling, hearing them talk in English.

'And tomorrow, your sisters and mother will come!'

The plates gleamed white and the sun moved in streaks across a sheer blue sea. A few boats, like small liners, were moored inside a distant breakwater.

'Ah yes, the Russians, rich men all.'

'Who knows?' The Englishman was grinning.

The father was hugging his son-in-law. A queer, hot peace hung about the beach, other French diners looked on at the scene. Zohre was smiling, they'd all moved on, merged into new positions that were more harmonious now.

Before the man and woman had talked together.

'We can both work here – it's fixed.'

'Yeah, maybe we needn't move for a while.' Back in England there'd been nothing. Here they'd been lucky, a language unit would take them on.

'There's no money in it.' The father was commenting. He

pointed to the ships moored in the offing. Then he grinned. 'But better than so.' They sat back, peaceful.

Somewhere a police radio phone was crackling, there were French voices, the throb of a police motor bike passing, there were systems here. The bike droned into the distance, they might be watched or not, now the sun was going down and black seeped up from a distant line of islands, white lights lit a jetty. He was holding Zohre, they'd made it through, this far. The heat burnt out of the dark, the restaurant lights flared dim on the sand. Other diners' voices came. She was smiling, they hadn't turned back, it was enough for her, things continued, the path ahead, with him, attracted her.